W9-BZZ-755

LIBRARY

WITHDRAWN

Camp Rules

Camp Rules

JORDAN ROTER

DUTTON BOOKS

Y ROT
Roter, Jordan
Camp rules
31332000013000

~ p (~~~) Inc.

Published by the Penguin Group
Penguin Group (USA) Inc., 375 Hudson Street, New York, New York 10014, U.S.A.
Penguin Group (Canada), 90 Eglinton Avenue East, Suite 700, Toronto, Ontario, Canada
M4P 2Y3 (a division of Pearson Penguin Canada Inc.) • Penguin Books Ltd, 80 Strand,
London WC2R ORL, England • Penguin Ireland, 25 St Stephen's Green, Dublin 2, Ireland
(a division of Penguin Books Ltd) • Penguin Group (Australia), 250 Camberwell Road,
Camberwell, Victoria 3124, Australia (a division of Pearson Australia Group Pty Ltd)
Penguin Books India Pvt Ltd, 11 Community Centre, Panchsheel Park, New Delhi - 110 017,
India • Penguin Group (NZ), 67 Apollo Drive, Mairangi Bay, Auckland 1311, New
Zealand (a division of Pearson New Zealand Ltd) • Penguin Books (South Africa) (Pty)
Ltd, 24 Sturdee Avenue, Rosebank, Johannesburg 2196, South Africa • Penguin Books Ltd,
Registered Offices: 80 Strand, London WC2R ORL, England

This book is a work of fiction. Names, characters, places, and incidents are either the product of
the author's imagination or are used fictitiously, and any resemblance to actual persons, living or
dead, business establishments, events, or locales is entirely coincidental.

Copyright © 2007 by Jordan Roter

All rights reserved. No part of this publication may be reproduced or transmitted in any form or
by any means, electronic or mechanical, including photocopying, recording, or any information
storage and retrieval system now known or to be invented, without permission in writing from
the publisher, except by a reviewer who wishes to quote brief passages in connection with a
review written for inclusion in a magazine, newspaper, or broadcast.

The publisher does not have any control over and does not assume any responsibility for author
or third-party websites or their content.

CIP Data is available.

Published in the United States by Dutton Books,
a member of Penguin Group (USA) Inc.
345 Hudson Street, New York, New York 10014
www.penguin.com/youngreaders

Designed by Abby Kuperstock

Printed in USA • First Edition
ISBN 978-0-525-47803-4
1 3 5 7 9 10 8 6 4 2

FEB 13 2009

Young adult
FICTION

177613

For all the girls in my life, with love

ACKNOWLEDGMENTS

Countless thanks to: all the lovely folks at Dutton who made this book possible, especially my beloved editor-slash-friend, Julie Strauss-Gabel.

(Captain) Richard Abate, Nicole Clemens, and Kate Lee.

Every member of my family, especially to my fabulous cousins—and fellow Tripp Lake Camp Ladies—Jill, Laura, and Amanda . . . And of course, to my parents for giving me the incredible gift of camp in the first place.

Guy . . . for being the best bunkmate a girl could ask for . . . I love your way.

And last but certainly not least, to all my girls, to whom this book is dedicated. . . . I am so very lucky to have each and every one of you in my life. You inspire me and rock my world on a daily basis. Thank you for your love, your laughter, and your friendship. Rock on, girls.

*   *   *

Camp Rules

CAMP RULE #1

Fern Lake ladies are eternally
grateful for the gift of camp.

On May 26, Penny Moore woke up for the very first
time . . . as a sixteen-year-old. She was still wearing what
she had gone to sleep in (when she was just *fif*teen): her
very worn-in, very old, very favorite Hello Kitty nightgown.
These days, she wore it with boys' drawstring pajama bottoms because the aforementioned favorite night*gown* now
ended at her waist. The material was soft and tissue-paper
thin from a decade of washing and wearing.

Her mother once tried to throw it out, which didn't
go over so well. Penny picked it out of the trash (and, yes,
there was tuna salad involved, but no, she couldn't bear to
discuss it ever again). Needless to say, Penny sterilized her
precious sleepwear, washing it several times. Some girls had
blankies or stuffed animals, Penny Moore had a nightgown.
A nightshirt. A nightgownshirt. *Whatever.*

So, just as her alarm went off on that very special, very pivotal birthday morning, Penny's parents barreled into her bedroom. They were whistling and singing "Sixteen Candles." Okay, it was cute. And really sweet. And she kind of wanted to sing along, but she hadn't even brushed her teeth yet! Not to mention the fact that she was sixteen now and it was time for her to assert her privacy rights!

"Um, helloooo? Ever heard of a little thing called 'knocking'?" she asked. Had they been standing outside the door just waiting for her alarm to go off? Probably. Penny's parents *were* very punctual. And surprisingly energetic—for parents, that is.

"You guys are so *weird*!!!" said Penny.

"Not as *weird* as you being SIXTEEN years old!" said Penny's mother. "Oh, my, that makes me . . ."

"A thousand?" Penny asked.

Penny and her mom stuck their tongues out at each other at the same time. They could both be superimmature sometimes.

"As beautiful as the day we met," said Penny's father.

And then, Penny's parents kissed each other. Unfortunately, that sort of thing seemed to happen quite often in the Moore household.

"Ew, guys! PDAs on my birthday? In my *room*? *Really?*"

"What are 'PDAs'?" asked Penny's mom.

"Public Displays of Affection," said Penny's dad. Penny's

mother looked at Penny's father, impressed. "What? I'm 'down' with the Y Gen jargon," he added proudly.

"Dad—"

"But we're not in public," said Penny's mom.

"I know, but she must think that if there's more than just the two of us in the room, that then—"

"Then, it's public, right. Got it," said Penny's mom. "But it's not, not really . . . public. Because we're at home. And then, wouldn't *Private* Displays of Affection have the same abbreviation anyway? PDA?"

"You make a strong point, Nancy," said Penny's dad.

"Who do I talk to about changing that abbreviation?" asked Penny's mom.

"Probably the same person I talk to about changing parents!"

"Did she just say what I think she just said?" asked Penny's mom.

"I don't know, Nance, maybe she doesn't want her birthday present?"

"Maybe she wants some . . . tickle torture?!"

Penny's mom lurched toward Penny. She knew exactly where to tickle Penny to make her laugh uncontrollably. Penny believed that her mother had programmed her tickle spots while she was still in the womb (which was a totally unfair advantage). But finally, Penny broke free and stopped the insanity.

"People! Please!" said Penny. "I am sixteen now! It is a whole new dawn. Let's have a little respect for the new age, shall we?"

Penny's parents looked at each other like they were going to burst out laughing. Penny was wondering why no one seemed to take her seriously?

"Sorry, honey. You're right."

Penny's mom swiftly grabbed a large white cardboard box with a green ribbon wrapped around it from behind Penny's father's back. Penny sat up and rubbed her hands together for what was sure to be the greatest birthday present. Ever.

"Oh my God, I know you got me those Seven jeans I wanted! You shouldn't have! They're like a hundred and fifty dollars!!!"

"A hundred and eighty, actually," said Penny's mom. "But you won't know what it is for sure until you look."

Penny's dad put his arm around Penny's mom, and they stared at their daughter expectantly, as if she were a baby who was about to speak her first word. She crossed her fingers, shut her eyes tightly, and made a silent wish for her jeans. She tore off the green ribbon, and the top of the white box, and the green tissue paper, only to find . . . a simple white collared shirt.

"What the . . ."

Penny didn't dare finish that sentence. Instead, she just stared at the shirt, and then at her parents, who looked like they were going to absolutely burst with excitement. What was she missing? She desperately rummaged through the box for the jeans to go with the shirt. Or the iPod to go with the shirt . . . or anything to go with the shirt! But Penny's parents had always taught her to be polite. So she took a breath before speaking in a very calm voice.

"Thanks for the shirt, Mom and Dad, but I have a bunch just like this—"

"Unfold it!" yelled Penny's mom.

"Oooookay . . ."

As ordered, Penny took the shirt out of the package and saw that on the upper right corner, there was a little round navy blue logo. It read FLC.

"Um, is this some new cutting-edge clothing line that I don't know of yet? I mean, I haven't seen any of the cool girls in school wearing it, so—"

"No, honey, that logo stands for Fern Lake Camp. You're going to sleepaway camp this summer!!!"

Penny's mother flailed her arms over her head in excitement and she hopped into the air, then plopped back down on Penny's bed and hugged her. Penny's dad made an obscenely loud, truly bizarre noise that Penny assumed was meant to sound like a bugle being blown. Penny was in shock. She was not in the mood for imaginary instruments at that moment. Her life as she knew it had just changed completely. And there was really only one thing she could say:

"WHAT HAVE YOU DONE?!"

"We know how you always wanted to go to camp, but we couldn't afford it until now!"

"Yeah, I wanted to go when I was *eight* and everyone was going for the very first summer . . . I'm *SIXTEEN!*" said Penny. "No one starts sleepaway camp at sixteen! That's what college is for!"

"We thought you would be thrilled! Dad got the big promotion, and we thought, because you work so hard in school and you've always had a summer job, that this would be the perfect gift."

"No! No! Don't you see what you're doing? You're feeding me to the lions! I'm a sheep to the sleepaway-slaughter! You've sold me down the river!"

"It's a lake, actually," said Penny's dad. "I mean, if you want to be technical about it," he added.

"Whatever!" said Penny. She took a deep breath. "The point is, people, that they're going to destroy me. Because moving and starting a whole new school in the last year wasn't enough? Now I've gotta go be the new girl in a tight-knit group of girls who have been together for like a hundred summers? I don't think that you guys understand what we're dealing with here. These camp girls have *private* groups on MySpace! No one has *private* groups on MySpace! That's the whole point of MySpace!"

"Well, if they don't want private groups on MySpace, why didn't they call it *Our*Space?" asked Penny's mom.

Why did Penny's parents always have to be so very clever? And then she saw it: the patented Nancy Moore chin quiver. Penny knew she was being bratty and she didn't want to have made her mom cry, but *come on . . . summer camp?* This was going to be social suicide. And so she started to cry. Both Moore girls cried. For different reasons, of course, but the tears were flowing, nonetheless.

"Why are *you* crying?" Penny asked. "You don't have to go be the dorky new girl in the wilderness for four weeks . . ."

Penny's parents looked at each other sheepishly.

"What?" asked Penny. "What's that look?"

"It's eight weeks," said Penny's father.

"*Eight* weeks?!"

"Seven and a half . . . technically."

"You're sending me away for seven and a half weeks? Do you just absolutely *hate* me?"

"Of course not! We love you, honey. We thought this was what you wanted. And we'll come up to see you on Visiting Day, and you'll introduce us to all your great new friends."

"Can't we just get your money back?"

"Honey, we already put our deposit down. It's nonrefundable."

"Please, I'm begging you! Don't do this. I will be scarred for life."

"That's exactly what you said about ballet, and you—"

"Tripped on my own foot and did a face plant into the hardwood floor. I got three stitches! I am *literally* scarred for life!"

"I'm really sorry you feel this way, honey. We did this for you. We just wanted to give you something you had always wanted."

"Yeah, I guess I'll be careful what I wish for from now on."

Penny rarely fought with her parents. Aside from them being parents, she had to admit they were pretty cool. But how else was she supposed to react to this surprise "birthday present"?

Penny never thought of herself as an ungrateful girl. In fact, she was just the opposite. At Lakefield Academy, where Penny had just started the previous year and was on partial scholarship, she snubbed (okay, they snubbed her, too) the New York City kids who were chauffered from their Fifth Avenue duplexes and Central Park West museumlike apartments to the school, nestled just blocks from where Penny lived. Penny usually took the bus, or walked if it was a nice day. Once in a while, if she was running late, her father would drop her off in his old station wagon. This was to be avoided at all costs, as he had a habit of honking the horn three times and waving vigorously the moment Penny exited the car.

"Hey, guys, can you make me one promise, please?"

"We're listening."

"When you come up for Visiting Day, if I'm still miserable, will you promise to let me come home with you?"

"Penny—"

"Please, just promise me. If I try it, if I try it for three weeks or four weeks or whatever it is, and camp just isn't for me . . . can I come home with you guys? Please?"

Penny's parents looked at each other. They shrugged their shoulders.

"I think that's a fair deal," said Penny's dad.

"I'm okay with that," said Penny's mom.

"Okay," said Penny. "Okay."

Penny nodded to herself. So that was it: Penny had one month to prepare (emotionally and physically) for Fern Lake Camp. And that's how Penny Moore went from Sweet Sixteen to Sucky Sixteen . . . in just under six minutes.

CAMP RULE #2

Fern Lake ladies love to express
themselves through cheer.

When the Moore family pulled up to the Delta terminal at New York's La Guardia airport, they saw a sea of white and navy blue, as throngs of young girls in Fern Lake Camp uniforms got out of their parents' cars, gathered their carry-on bags, and entered the terminal.

"We're heeeeeeeeeeeeeere!" said Penny's father.

"Greeeeeeeeeeaaaaaaaaaaat," said Penny.

Penny was officially and overwhelmingly underenthused. She watched as most of the younger girls clung to their parents. The older girls squealed and screamed. They ran from their parents—often dropping their carry-ons, lacrosse sticks, and tennis rackets in the process—and literally jumped all over their friends. Penny looked down at her own uniform. To the naked eye, she imagined that she looked like she could be "one of them." *I can do this*, she told herself silently. But at that moment, she wasn't sure she would even be able to extricate herself from the car with any kind of composure, as her legs had fallen asleep way back at Exit Fifty-six.

And then a very shiny, very flashy, very huge black Rolls-Royce pulled up in front of them. A driver wearing a chauffeur suit and cap got out and opened the door for a girl with blond highlights, who slowly emerged from the car. Penny was momentarily blinded as the sun glinted off the triangular Prada label on the girl's large black tote. There was a palpable hush among the crowd. As Penny's vision slowly restored, she noticed that the girl seemed to be wearing the same FLC uniform as everyone else: navy blue shorts, and a white collared shirt. But it looked different on her. It looked perfect. *She* looked perfect. *Did she have it tailored maybe?* Penny could tell, just by looking at this girl from the back and just for a second, which table she would sit at in the high school caf, and for sure it would not be hers.

"That's Logan Worthe," said one girl to her parents.

Did she just say Logan Worthe? THE Logan Worthe? The Logan Worthe who ruled Lakefield Academy, Penny's high school? Logan Worthe not only ruled the school, but she was also the leader of the Fab Four, the most popular girls at Lakefield Academy. She was notorious throughout the City: she dated any boy she wanted (or so everyone said), she bought any clothes she wanted (or so it seemed), and she threw all the wild parties she wanted (not that Penny had ever been invited).

"Did you see Logan Worthe?" asked one camper. "She's, like, the coolest girl in Bunk One."

Logan Worthe was smiling broadly. Penny knew that smile. Logan Worthe was everywhere, it seemed. She was always composed, always cool, always . . . Logan Worthe. But why, if she was such a sophisticated wild child, was she still going to an all-girls sleepaway camp at sixteen years old? And why did it have to be the same one as Penny?

Logan walked with utmost confidence toward the sliding glass doors of the terminal, but before she could enter she was approached by a group of girls.

"Hi, Logan," said one young camper.

"Ellie! How *are* you?"

"Oh my God! She remembered my name," squealed the camper to her equally Logan-obsessed friend.

Logan gave them both big hugs. Logan's warm reception toward Ellie seemed to embolden some of the other young campers. Penny noted that camp-Logan seemed much nicer, more affectionate, and certainly more approachable than school-Logan. Throngs of girls came over to pay their respects to Logan, who might as well have been FLC's answer to the Godfather. She was gracious—like a seasoned celebrity greeting her fans—as girls quickly surrounded her.

"Where are your parents?" asked one camper.

"Candace and Lloyd were unable to drive me because they left for St. Tropez yesterday," replied Logan. "James drives me to the plane every year. It's kind of like our little tradition."

Logan winked at James. *Oh, please. St. Tropez? Chauffeur? Calling her own parents by their first names? It's called perspective: try getting some.* Penny looked around to see if anyone else found this as obnoxious as she did, but it seemed they were all too busy worshipping Logan Worthe to notice.

"Have a great summer, James!" she said. "See you in August!"

"Yes, indeed, Miss Logan. Have fun!"

"I always do!"

Logan smiled her perfect Logan Worthe smile and waved as James drove away. Penny was officially in shock.

"Nancy, why don't you go with Penny?" said Penny's father. "I'll park and come meet you."

"I'm okay. You can really just drop me off here," said Penny.

"Drop you off on the side of the road like an abandoned child? I think not!"

"A little melodramatic, don't you think, Nan?"

"But she's my baby!"

Alert! Alert! Chin quiver! Penny figured she had about forty, maybe forty-five seconds, to get out of the car until a full-on crying eruption—which would inevitably make Penny start to cry. And Penny wasn't sure she even had any tears left after last night's private crying session into her nightgownshirt; it was still a little damp.

"I'm outta here, people," said Penny. "Unless, of course, you want to scratch this whole camp thing?"

And that's about when Penny's mom lost it.

"Oh, Mom. Please don't cry. I'm sorry, I'm just. Scared. Superscared. I'm terrified."

"But they look like very nice girls," said Penny's mom through tears.

"You're right," said Penny. "They totally do. I mean, I'm sure they are . . . nice. Mom, I love you. And I need you to get out of your seat so that I can get out."

Penny's mom slowly got out of the car. Penny pushed the seat forward and climbed out, slinging her old green backpack over her shoulder. Penny's mother put the second strap over Penny's other shoulder. OPERATION: DORK OUT YOUR DAUGHTER *has been completed.*

"Take the bull by the horns, Penny!" said Penny's mom.

"What?" Penny asked.

"Oh, I don't know. I got carried away," said Penny's mom.

"And don't forget your promise, okay?" asked Penny.

"We won't," said Penny's father.

"Visiting Day or bust!" yelled Penny's mom.

Penny hugged her parents tightly and wiped away a bur-
geoning tear when they weren't looking. They said "I love
you" to each other about a hundred more times until the
airport security guard had to pry them apart and threaten
to ticket Penny's father.

Penny waved as her parents drove off, and she walked
through the sliding glass doors at the same moment Logan
Worthe was entering the terminal to a duet of squeals.

"SIS BOOM BAH LOGAN RAH!" yelled one camper.

"SIS BOOMEDY HOORAH, JADE!" replied Logan.

Logan ran to Jade and gave her a huge hug. Jade's light
brown hair, with black tips, was in a ponytail.

"Rah rah, Willow!" said Logan.

Willow was sitting Indian style on the floor of the airport, calmly reading a book. Willow's superlong, down-
to-her-butt and naturally shiny auburn hair was tied into
loose pigtails, and dangling from a string around her neck
she wore a peace sign made of bark.

"Bum buddy bum bum, Logan!" said Willow.

Willow put down her book and joined the two girls in
midhug. They started to stomp their feet and squeal.

"How was the trip, Will?" asked Logan.

"It was really wonderful, Logee. Asia was beautiful,
and I learned so much about myself. I think maybe I was a
samurai in a past life. Anyway, I had some chamomile tea on
the plane, and it was just so soothing that I couldn't help

but doze off. I love sleeping on airplanes . . . it's like . . . float-ing on a cloud, you know?"

"Call me when the shuttle lands," said Jade.

Willow punched her in the arm.

"Ow," said Jade. "For a hippie, you sure know how to pack a punch."

"I'm a hippelectual," replied Willow. "It's a hybrid of a hippie and an intellectual, if you must know."

"I thought you didn't believe in labeling because it was derivative?" asked Logan.

"This is true. But if I make it up, then it's unique. Like me!" Willow smiled and made a peace sign with her fingers as she stuck out her tongue.

A pretty blond girl and her mother entered the termi-nal, but neither seemed to notice Penny, even though they were standing right next to her. In fact, no one seemed to notice Penny at all. Penny Moore was, for all intents and purposes, invisible. Which was not a brand-new experience for Penny, but still, this kind of instant invisibility was a little excessive, even for her.

"Sis boom bah, Bunk One rah!" cheered the blond camper.

"Tess, please keep your voice down," said Tess's mother, her palm pressed lightly on her left ear.

Tess had a tennis racket bag over her shoulder. She wore her hair in a tight ponytail (with a couple stubborn blond curls loose around her face), and her sneakers had light pink pom-poms sticking out the back.

"Sorry, Mummy," said Tess.

"OH. MY. GOD! I can NOT believe we are here!" screamed another girl from the doorway of the terminal. "That's right, we're here, we're Bunk One, get used to it! Bunk One *rocks!*"

"Yes, hello, Gabby," said Tess's mother. "I see she still lives on Long Island."

"Mummy!" said Tess.

"Gabby! Would you please come over here and help your father and myself with your stuff? You always do this! What am I gonna do with you?" said Gabby's mother, in a thick Long Island accent.

"Sorry, Ma," said Gabby. She rolled her eyes.

The girls ran over to hug Gabby before she went to help her parents. Penny noted that these girls seemed to move more comfortably in a pack. She looked down at their sneakers: they were each wearing brand-new Nikes in different bright colors. They must have designed them themselves, because the back of each girl's left sneaker read BUNK, and the back of each right sneaker read ONE.

"*Bunk One?*" Penny said, reading the sneakers aloud.

"Okay, Fern Lake ladies," boomed a tiny adult in a Fern Lake uniform. "I'm Stacy, and I am the Fern Lake Camp head counselor."

Logan Worthe and her friends launched into song. The other campers joined right in with them.

> *"We love you, Stacy,*
> *Oh yes we do,*
> *We love you, Stacy,*
> *And we'll be true.*
> *When you're not with us, we're blue-oo-oo,*
> *Oh, Stacy, we love you!"*

"That's nice, girls," said Stacy. "It is now time to say good-bye to your parents. Parents, please say good-bye to your daughters so that we can all move through airport security in a timely fashion."

Ironically, while this Stacy-woman was tiny in stature, she had the inordinately loud and low (and utterly monotone) voice of a male giant. The combination was highly disconcerting. She proudly carried an overflowing clipboard, which proved to Penny that if you give just about anyone a clipboard, they become—or at the very least, look—terribly official.

Campers and parents hugged and kissed and cried, and Penny realized she was just about the only camper who had insisted on being dropped off curbside. So Penny looked at her nails (they were short), and put her hands in her pockets (they were shallow), and tried to blend in with the other campers (even though she was sure she stood out like a sore, parent-less thumb).

Tess's mother air-kissed her and put her hand on her daughter's shoulder.

"Now, Tess, remember to play tennis every day. You have all the workouts your trainer gave you?"

"Yes, Mummy," said Tess.

Gabby's mother and father hugged her together. Gabby's mom gave her a big kiss on the cheek, and then gruffly used her thumb to wipe off the lipstick mark she had left there. She hugged her again.

"Ugh, I miss you already!" said Gabby's mother. "I always forget how hard this is!"

"Ma, stop manhandling me, you're like crushing me . . . Ma, I can't breathe, *gasp*!"

"Ugh! Would you look at this punim?!"

Gabby's mother squeezed Gabby's cheeks.

"Ow! Ma, those are my cheeks . . . I need those!" said Gabby. "Love you guys . . . see you on Visiting Day!"

The girls then hooked arms and literally skipped through airport security. *Who skips through airport security?* Penny could have sworn they even cheered the metal detector. When they weren't cheering loudly, they were whispering loudly, so Penny could hear almost every word.

"Do you guys remember Deborah Fischer?" whispered Logan. "Can you believe she is *still* not wearing a bra?"

"I'm not wearing a bra," said Willow.

"You have no boobs, Will . . . and you burned yours in a campfire last year when they confiscated your hemp blanket."

"Come on, Logan, let's try to practice some tolerance this summer," said Willow.

"Tolerance is so . . . bourgeois."

"Well, you better get pretty cozy with bourgeois if you want to finally win that spirit award this year," said Gabby.

"Rah rah, Deborah." Logan rolled her eyes. "Hi, Tracy, how *are* you?"

Logan squealed as she hugged another little girl who could now die a very happy camper because Logan Worthe had acknowledged her.

Penny adjusted her loose uniform shirt self-consciously. She was not wearing a bra either. Fortunately or unfortunately, Penny Moore's chest (or lack thereof) was literally flat as a board. She owned a couple of "training" bras that her mother had bought for her, but she never seemed to find any that fit her right, or were comfortable at all, so most of the time she didn't wear anything.

"No bombs in those bags, right, girls?" Stacy asked. She laughed heartily at her own joke.

The girls laughed politely while elbowing and pinching one another. The airport security guards must not have found Stacy's joke so funny, because they pulled her to the side to frisk her and give her a speech about the seriousness of airport security. The girls found this hilarious, and started laughing. Willow sneezed.

"Are you allergic to humor now, Willow?"

"Jade. Be nice," said Logan.

"I was kidding!"

"Peace, girls. It's our last summer!" said Willow.

"Girls, remember, you're Bunk One now. You have to set the example this summer," said Stacy.

It was a bit hard to take her seriously at that moment, considering that she was standing with her legs spread and her shoes off as she was being frisked by one guard, while another was rifling relentlessly through her bag and beloved clipboard.

"Let's show everyone how Fern Lake ladies behave!" continued Stacy.

"Keep your hands on the wall, miss!" barked the security guard.

Gabby used her hand and her armpit to make a farting noise.

"Nice touch," said Logan.

"Achoo!" sneezed Willow.

"Let me guess . . ."

"Allergies," said all the girls at once.

"Yeah."

"Maybe you should reconsider the hemp bag then, no?"

"Yeah, hemp: not the best for hay fever."

"I got these Chinese herbs that I'm supposed to—"

But before Willow could finish the sentence, she sneezed again. This time, she turned her head toward Penny. Since both Willow's hands were filled with her belongings, she sneezed all over her. Penny closed her eyes as she felt a wet spray hit her face and arms. Willow had some real torque on those sneezes.

"Oh my God! Oh . . . my . . . I am so sorry," said Willow. "Here, take this." She dug a (potentially used) handkerchief out of her shorts pocket.

Penny opened her eyes one at a time.

"Thanks, but I'll just go to the bathroom."

"I'm really sorry," said Willow. "I just, I had no hands, and I have these allergies, and that sneeze just snuck up on me. It's like that ancient Chinese proverb, oh, how does it go?"

"It's not a day until you sneeze . . . during it?" asked Penny.

"I don't think that was it," said Willow. "But it was something like that."

"It's just allergies," said Gabby. "It's not like she has SARS or anything."

All the girls took a step back, and Tess put her hand over Gabby's mouth.

"What?" mumbled a muffled Gabby.

"I'm sorry," chirped Willow again.

"It's okay *REALLY*," said Penny.

Penny took her arm out of the second strap of her backpack and headed toward the bathroom. She didn't look back, but she could hear the girls whispering behind her.

"God, it's not like you, like, puked on her," said Jade.

"Wait, *do* you have SARS?" asked Gabby. "You can tell me. We're all camp friends here."

"I am not even going to dignify that with a response."

"That girl looked familiar. She looks kind of like a girl who goes to my *school*," said Logan. "But the girl I'm thinking of is our age and, like, 'walks among dorks,' catch my drift?"

"She probably just looks older," said Tess.

"Yes, some girls aren't as 'well-preserved' as you, Logan," said Jade.

"I feel bad," said Willow.

"Don't," said Jade. "She totally overreacted."

"You guys, who cares?! We're going back to camp!!!" said Gabby.

And just before Penny entered the ladies' room, she heard the girls start to sing gleefully in unison while clapping:

"I want to go back to Fern Lake Camp,
In dear old Pitsmouth, Maine!"

Penny rolled her eyes, and entered the bathroom quietly singing:

"I don't want to go to Mean Girl Camp in dear old
Nowheresville!"

Penny put her hands under the faucet. The water started automatically, and she splashed it on her face. She looked at herself in the dirty mirror—at her messy hair, and her now damp uniform—as she pumped the pink liquid soap from the dispenser. She had the overwhelming feeling that she was going to need a lot of Purell this summer if the first five minutes was any indication. She went to grab some paper towels and then realized the dispenser was empty. *Great.* Penny went into one of the stalls to grab some toilet paper instead. But as she tried to roll the stubborn dispenser (and was about to start clawing it with her fingernails in desperation and frustration), she heard something coming from the adjacent stall. It sounded distinctly like crying. She looked under the divider to see a pair of tiny and pristinely white Keds. She heard the sound of a nose being blown. She knocked lightly on the stall.

"You okay in there?" asked Penny.

No answer. She tried again.

"Hello? Are you okay?"

Suddenly, the shoes disappeared, and then a moment later, the top of a little head (framed by two hands clasped over the edge of the wall) popped up out of the stall. She was wearing immensely thick glasses, and had an eye patch over one eye.

"No," she said.

"Oh." That wasn't the answer Penny had been hoping for. Frankly, it was kind of a conversation stopper. Nevertheless, Penny tried again. "Do you want to talk about it?"

"No," she said.

She disappeared behind the wall again. Penny stood still. She didn't know how to respond. "No" was usually pretty definitive. But just as Penny was about to leave the bathroom, the voice continued.

"I don't want to go to camp."

Finally, a voice of reason! "Join the club," said Penny.

The head attached to the voice popped up again. Penny detected that she spoke with a touch of a lisp.

"You don't want to go either?" she asked. "But you're a big girl. I thought big girls loved camp. That's what my mom said."

"That's funny," said Penny. "That's what my mom said, too."

"Were they both lying?"

"No, I mean . . . every girl is different, I guess. Is this your first summer?"

"Yeah."

"Me too," said Penny.

"Wow. You're really old to be a new camper."

"Thanks."

"Are you scared?" asked the little girl.

"Terrified."

"Really?"

"Really," Penny replied.

"Have you ever been away from home before?"

"Nope."

"Me either. How old are you?"

"Sixteen. You?"

"Nine."

"Nine years old," Penny said thoughtfully. "Let me think . . . I remember liking age nine: it's the pinnacle of the single digits, so you're not yet encumbered by the double digits of it all. I'm not going to lie, nine is a strong age."

"Really?"

"Absolutely," said Penny. "So, do you mind my asking why you're wearing an eye patch?"

"My brother hit me with a hard hockey puck and I can't see out of my right eye."

"That had to hurt."

"Yeah. It was an accident. I have to wear the patch for a few more weeks though."

"I like it. I think the patch works. It's really . . . cool."

"Really?"

At that moment, there was an announcement over the crackly airport loudspeaker that their flight was boarding. Penny's stomach dropped into the dirty bathroom floor, and she was afraid she might throw up a little. But she didn't want this little kid to see "the big girl" puke. So she played it cool.

"That's our flight. What's your name?" asked Penny.

"Morgan."

"Morgan, I'm Penny."

"Hi."

"Hi."

"So, should we make a run for it?" asked Morgan.

"Nah, I think we should try it out," said Penny. "You never know, maybe it will be fun. Come on, let's get you cleaned up and get on the plane."

Penny didn't really believe what she was saying, but luckily, it seemed as though Morgan did. Morgan then tumbled off the toilet she had been standing on and hit the floor with an audible crash.

"Morgan, are you okay?"

"Yeah," said Morgan. "It happens a lot."

She unlocked the bolt on her stall, and hit herself in the head with the door as she opened it.

"Ow."

"It really does happen a lot, doesn't it?"

"Yeah."

Even Penny had to admit that between Morgan's short bowl-like hair, the eye patch, the glasses, and her very ill-fitting uniform, she looked like a complete train wreck. Not that Penny would have said that to her, of course. Morgan came up to Penny's hip when she stood next to her at the sink. She washed her hands, and then Penny handed her some toilet paper.

"Thanks, Penny," said Morgan, drying her hands. "Will you sit with me on the plane?"

"Sure, I'd love to."

"I brought playing cards. And gummy bears. But my mom says I'm not allowed to eat more than ten at a time or I get a headache."

"Morgan, I have a feeling you're going to do just fine at FLC."

Penny put her arm around Morgan's shoulders. And just like that, Penny Moore had made her first friend. She was nine years old, and she had an eye patch.

You have to start somewhere.

CAMP RULE #3

Fern Lake ladies share meaning-
ful precamp correspondences with
their designated camp-big-sisters
(i.e., they do not SPAM block
precamp e-mails!).

Once the guards released Stacy from airport security, the girls boarded the plane. The ride was only an hour, but to Penny it seemed like forever. Maybe because she was still in shock? Or maybe because the cheers the girls were singing (or, more aptly, screaming) hurt her ears more than the fluctuating cabin pressure. It felt like Penny had stepped into a super-duper cheerful cult!

It was pretty clear to Penny that Stacy was terrified of flying. She kept her clipboard clutched to her chest while still trying (and simultaneously, failing) to look authoritative. Penny sat next to Morgan, who got her hand caught in between the seats, and then tripped over her own seat belt on the way to the bathroom. She almost choked on her gummy bears, which she generously shared with Penny. For

Penny, the gummy bears were by far the highlight of her summer camp experience thus far.

When the pilot announced that they were landing in Portland, Maine, the campers squealed with excitement. Penny looked out the window as they came through the clouds, and it finally dawned on her: there was no way out now. Whether she liked it or not, she was officially a Fern Lake lady.

There was a cheering lull from 3:42 P.M. until 3:44 P.M. eastern standard time. Penny clocked it. But after the girls disembarked from the plane and settled onto the bus, the cheers began again. Penny sat next to the window with Morgan beside her, neither one of them knowing the words to any of the thousands of cheers and songs being sung around them.

After about an hour of this, Logan stood up, donned a huge smile, and gave a perfunctory clap.

"Okay, girls, we should be arriving at FLC in approximately T minus five minutes. So, if you'll all sing with me, 'Thunderrrrrr . . .'"

The girls started singing quietly with her:

"Thunder, thunderation.
We're the best camp in the nation.
When we fight with determination,
We create a great sensation."

They repeated this cheer, getting a little louder with each verse, until they were stomping their feet and yelling at the top of their lungs. Penny looked out the window and tried to tune out the screams.

"Fern Lake Road! There it is!" yelled Jade.

All the campers moved to one side of the bus to get a better view. Penny was sure the bus was going to tip. She kept staring out the window while the "Thundera-tion" chanting degenerated into loud primal screaming and tone-deaf yells as Fern Lake came into view from the road. She could see a rolling hill lined with grass, playing fields, and tennis courts that all led down to what must have been Fern Lake, and the modest white buildings that peppered the grounds. Okay, Penny had to admit: it was pretty. It was very green. And pretty. Cool! Could she go home now?

"The promised land!" one camper shouted.

On the bus, there were many tears. There was much hug-ging. There was hyper-hyperventilation. There was some sweating. One girl fanned the other. It was chaos, utter and total ebullient chaos.

The bus came to a stop at the head of campus. From Penny's seat by the window, she could see a man and a woman in camp uniforms (the man's kneesocks were actu-ally pulled up to his knees). Penny recognized the petite blond woman and the doofy-looking-kneesock man from the camp DVD her parents had played for her. They were the camp owners, Barbara and George. There was a little boy standing with them who had a huge grin on his face as he watched the girls swarming around him.

Other girls who had already arrived at camp waited impatiently behind Barb and George, who functioned as a human barricade simply by the force of their adult presence. Penny watched as girls of every height and shape (all dressed in the identical uniform) scoured the bus in attempts to find their friends. In the meantime, they waved and yelled indiscriminately. Some waited with their arms around each other screaming and crying, others broke free and ran alongside of the bus as it was pulling to a stop. Some of the campers reached their hands out the bus window to the girls on the ground even though they couldn't actually reach them.

While Penny didn't necessarily understand the chaos, it was pretty clear that all the crying and the screaming was that of pure, unadulterated joy and anticipation. Stacy stood up in the front, clutching her clipboard. The girls immediately launched into song again:

> *"Her name is Stacy*
> *We love her so much it's craCy*
> *Stacy, you organize the schedule*
> *And you don't let us meddle*

Stacy Stacy
We will try not to drive you cracy cracy!
Sis boomedy hoorah, Stacy!"

Stacy smiled semitolerantly.

"Welcome back to Fern Lake, girls."

"Sis boomedy hoorah, Fern Lake!"

"Girls, if you want to get off this bus, and into your bunks, I'm going to need just a few minutes of silence to give you your bunk assignments. New campers: the counselors and returning campers are here to help you find your bunks. The bunks are organized in numerically descending order in a circle around the flagpole."

Stacy started calling out names from her clipboard. Every time she called out that one of the girls was to be in Bunk One, the girls would cheer her from their seats in the front of the bus, just ahead of where Penny was sitting.

"Furlong, Jade: Bunk One."

"Sis boomedy hoorah, Jade!"

"Harkness, Willow: Bunk One."

"Sis boomedy hoorah, Willow!"

Willow dabbed her eyes with her tissue and dipped her head as she wiped away a tear. Logan put her arm around her neck.

"Allergies," said Willow.

"Yeah, right," said Logan. "Me too."

Penny craned her neck and looked through the space between the two seats in front of her. Logan used the side of her index finger to wipe away a tear from her left eye. Penny was surprised to see Logan Worthe shedding a tear. *Popular girls cry, too?*

"Steinberg, Gabby: Bunk One."

Gabby jumped out of her seat with both her arms raised over her head.

"YES!" she yelled. "YESSSSSSSSSSSSSSS!"

"Vanderbank, Tess: Bunk One."

"Sis boomedy hoorah, Tess!"

Tess silently (yet triumphantly) raised one arm straight up in the air, her hand in a fist.

"Worthe, Logan: Bunk One."

"Sis boomedy hoorah, Logan!"

They cheered themselves once again and hugged some more.

"Moore, Penny."

Penny watched Logan perk up. Morgan looked at her expectantly. Penny slouched down into her seat and put her index finger to her lips, shushing her. Penny thought about this thing she once saw on the nature channel about a lizard that could completely blend into any background when it was in distress. Oh, how she wanted to be that lizard at that moment. *Distress! Distress! Be the lizard!*

"Penny Moore!" said Logan. "That's my Camp Little

Sister who never e-mailed me back . . . so rude . . . could you imagine? I am, like, such a Camp Big Sister score!"

"And so modest, too," said Jade.

"Whatever," replied Logan. "I wonder what the little flake looks like."

Little sister? Logan Worthe was Penny's Camp Big Sister? Penny had read about this in the brochure, that every new camper gets an older "big sister" to look after her, but as far as Penny knew, she was never contacted. *Did Penny SPAM block an e-mail from the most popular girl in school (and now, camp)?*

"Penny Moore. Bunk One," said Stacy.

"Sis boom—" started Gabby.

Logan whacked Gabby in the arm.

"Ow!" she yelped. "What's your *damage?*"

Penny didn't breathe for a solid thirty seconds. There was silence on the bus. Morgan looked up at Penny in awe. Penny shook her head, warning Morgan not to dare break the silence. Like maybe if Penny was really quiet, no one would figure out who she was . . . *the entire summer.*

Logan stood up from her seat and raised her hand, but didn't wait for Stacy to acknowledge her before speaking.

"I'm sorry, Stacy, but—"

"Logan Worthe, is there a problem?"

"Well, yes, first of all, hello, everyone! And welcome to Fern Lake," said Logan sweetly to the whole bus. And then she turned and whispered into Stacy's ear. "I think you misspoke. You said something about a 'Penny Moore' being in Bunk One?"

Stacy searched her clipboard, puzzled.

"You're right, Logan!" said Stacy. "Now, how did that mistake happen?"

Stacy continued to search through her clipboard as Logan led Bunk One in a group sigh of relief.

"Whew! That was a little scary, Stacy," said Logan.

"Tell me about it," said Stacy. "I spent all night putting these names into alphabetical order! How did Moore come out last?"

"Um, no, Stacy, see, this Penny Moore person is my *little* sister. Who, BTW, never even e-mailed me back, which is *so* un-Fern Lake lady-ish if you ask me! Anyway, you said that she was in Bunk One. Which you know, must be a mistake, because no one comes for their first year into Bunk One. I mean, everyone knows that!"

Stacy licked her finger and used it to dramatically flip back to the top page on her clipboard.

"Penny Moore?" she called.

Penny wanted to crawl under her seat. She wanted to disappear. She wanted to be anywhere but there. She was startled as Logan started laughing uncontrollably.

"Oh my god, Stacy! I get it! That's hilarious! Girls, it's a fake out! Of course! You totally got us!"

The girls started laughing together, relieved.

"Of course! A fake out! They are really getting kooky this summer!" said Tess.

"Kooky!"

"Seriously, could you imagine? A new girl in Bunk One? What a disaster!"

"I gotta hand it to you, you guys are thorough! You must have started planning this months ago. Wow. Nice work. You really got us," said Logan. "But I mean, couldn't you think of a better name than Penny Moore? It's so clearly made up!"

"Penny Moore, please stand up," said Stacy, unamused.

So, Penny stood up—or crouched up, considering the low ceiling of the bus. She tried to smile, and held up her hand to wave, but then thought better of it, even though she had already started the wave, so she imagined it looked like she had some kind of weird, momentary arm spasm. Everyone was looking at her. She might as well have had three heads. And if she did have three heads, Penny hoped that one of them would learn the cheers . . . fast.

"Here," croaked Penny.

"Bunk One," said Stacy.

Logan's smile faded slowly until it looked like she was actually going to explode or cry . . . or both. She looked at Penny as if she might strangle her with Willow's bark peace-sign necklace or Tess's blue-and-white Fern Lake lanyard. The other girls must have been in shock because they all just stared. Gabby's fluorescent green gum tumbled out of her gapingly open mouth.

"Gabby Steinberg, I'll be confiscating that gum, if you don't mind."

"But what about the two-second rule?"

"The two-second rule does not apply to food and/or candy, which is contraband," said Stacy.

Gabby sighed, picked her gum up off the floor of the bus, and put it in Stacy's outstretched hand.

"But, Stacy, she can't be in Bunk One with us . . . this is our last summer . . . this is what we have been waiting for our ENTIRE lives!"

"Well, Logan, you're just going to have to make do with one new camper in your bunk. You're not really showing her the Fern Lake spirit."

"But—"

"Miss Worthe! Sit down. Do I make myself clear?" Stacy was still holding Gabby's fluorescent green gum in her open hand.

"So much for finally winning that spirit award," whispered Jade.

"Shut it, Jade," said Logan. "Besides, maybe my little outburst is good. Ever heard the allegory of the prodigal son? It's the one who actually improves, the one who changes from bad to good, who is rewarded."

"I don't remember them giving an award for the prodigal camper," said Willow.

Logan sat down and glared at Penny over her shoulder.

"Miss Moore, you can sit down," said Stacy.

Penny sat. Could she go home now? she wondered. Maybe tomorrow? This was all clearly a huge mistake. A mix-up. A blunder. The mood on the bus was significantly more subdued after Logan's outburst, although there was plenty of whispering among the girls.

"Welcome," said Stacy, when she was finished announcing the bunk assignments.

It didn't sound very welcoming to Penny. She gave Morgan a hug as she walked to the door of the bus.

"Just be careful going down the steps," said Penny.

"Penny, will you please come visit me? I'm in Bunk Fourteen-A."

"Definitely, Morgan. And you can always come see me in . . ."

"Bunk One. Wow. Penny, you're great."

"I'm glad someone thinks so."

And then Morgan fell off the bus.

"Morgan!"

"I'm okay!" she said, brushing herself off. "And Penny? Thanks."

Penny smiled and watched as Morgan walked bravely to her bunk. She looked back at Penny and waved just before she tripped up her front stairs and disappeared inside. And then all of a sudden, Penny felt a painful *THUD!*

"Oops! Sorry! I'm so sorry! Are you okay?"

Tess had accidentally hit Penny in the head with her tennis racket bag as she tossed it over her shoulder.

"Yes," Penny said. "No problem."

"This thing should come with its own warning label!" said Tess.

Penny laughed too loudly at Tess's joke. Penny was consciously overcompensating for her intense lameness. She watched as Tess and the other Bunk Oners sprinted toward their infamous bunk. Penny looked at the circle of bunks around the flagpole and noted that Bunk One was the biggest and the closest one to the head of campus. She followed the other girls at a safe distance.

"I could help you with your bag."

When Penny turned around to see the face to match the voice, she saw no one . . . no one at her eye level, that was. She looked down, and there he was: the boy she had seen from the bus. He stared at Penny intently as he took a long slurp from his grape juice box.

"Name's Paxton," he said. "I could help you with your luggage if you ask me nicely. I'm stronger than I look."

"Hi. Name's Penny. I think I got it, but thanks."

Paxton followed Penny as she walked toward her new summer digs. *How cute*, thought Penny, *a ministalker*.

"Penny. Cool name. Like the coin. I like it. Pennies are lucky."

"I could challenge you on that theory right about now."

Penny had heard all the requisite penny jokes before. In fact, when she was younger, she threatened her parents that she was going to change her name to Cheryl. Penny thought maybe Paxton would get the hint to skedaddle as she walked up the steps to Bunk One. But, not so much . . .

"Bunk One, huh?" asked Paxton, trailing after Penny. "I like older women. I'm seven. Be eight in February. Aquarius: the water bearer. My parents own this camp. One day it'll be all mine." He laughed loudly and maniacally and then stopped as abruptly as he had started. "But for now, I'm just here to help. Give me a call if you get homesick."

Paxton pulled a scrap of paper out of his pocket and gave it to Penny. It had his name written on it in blue crayon.

"Thanks, Paxton," she said. She stuffed it in the pocket of her navy shorts, which—as a side note—had been giving her a serious wedgie all day.

"You can call me Paco. That's what most of the girls call me, anyway. You'll see, I'm kind of the camp 'man-scot.' So, what are you doing later?"

"Um, I don't really know . . . Paco."

"That's cool, Penny," he said. He looked around and then leaned in toward her conspiratorially. "Just know, I'm the guy behind the guy behind the guy who can get you into candy canteen, catch my drift?"

"Paxton! What are you doing *now*?" yelled Barbara.

"Be right there, Mom," he said. "Don't be a stranger."

He winked at Penny.

"Uh, thanks," she replied. "Or, I won't . . . be . . . a stranger."

This was getting weirder by the second. Did Penny just get hit on at an all-girls camp by a seven-year-old boy? She looked up at the white bunk in front of her. She was already standing on the steps leading to the front door. She looked up to see a wooden plaque that read simply in capital letters: BUNK ONE.

CAMP RULE #4

Fern Lake ladies wait their whole camp lives to reach the inner sanctum of Bunk One. New campers, please knock first.

Bunk One's flimsy wooden front door had a loose tin latch, which Penny was just about to unhook, when the door flew open toward her, hitting her in the forehead and pushing her down the stairs. So far, Penny's camp experience was more like a roller derby . . . without the roller skates.

"Oh my god! Are you okay?"

Penny put her hand on her forehead, which had taken the brunt of the hit (luckily, it could now counterbalance the bruise from Tess's tennis racket bag). Logan's face appeared directly in front of Penny's.

"Oh. It's *you*," said Logan. "What were you doing just standing there anyway?"

"I . . . was coming inside."

"Oh, that's right. Because this is '*your*' bunk?" Logan used her fingers to further emphasize that the word *your* was in quotations. "Well, I'll see you in there then. *Penny*. Wait a second. Have we met before?"

"I don't think so," Penny lied.

"Do you live in the City?"

Penny found it fascinating that New York City kids seemed to always refer to New York as "the City," as if there were no other cities in the United States, or the world for that matter.

"No, I live in the Bronx," said Penny.

"I go to school in the Bronx. Lakefield Academy. Maybe you've heard of it?"

There was no getting out of it now.

"Yeah, I go there, too," said Penny.

"*You* go to Lakefield? I thought you looked familiar!"

"I've only been there a year, but it seems like a really nice place to—"

"So you know who I am?"

"Well, yeah . . . I mean, everyone knows who you are."

"And who am I?"

"You're Logan Worthe. You basically run Lakefield."

"Unbelievable!" said Logan. She grabbed Penny's wrist and pulled her into a cramped space between Bunk One and the neighboring bunk where no one could see them. "Listen, Penny, I don't expect you to understand this, but things are different here. I'm not the same person at camp that I am at school."

"Okay . . ."

"But you are, only in that, you don't concern me. I prefer to leave this high school caste system crap in the tristate area, but you have single-handedly forced me to bring that element into the Promised Land. And for that, I will never forgive you."

Logan started to walk away. Tears were welling up in Penny's eyes and she was so tired and so upset and, well, this wasn't high school anymore and who cared what any of these girls thought of her? So she yelled back.

"I don't even want to be at your stupid camp anyway!"

It was not the most mature, nor the most articulate, sentence ever to come out of Penny's mouth, but it certainly got her point across because Logan stopped in her tracks, and slowly turned to face Penny.

"What did you just say?" she asked.

"I don't want to be at your stupid camp," said Penny (with considerably less conviction).

"Looks like we have something in common after all. I don't want you to be here, and you don't want you to be here. So why don't you just go home, Penny?"

"Please! I would love to go home. But I can't. My parents forced me to come here and won't let me go home. I'm stuck here. Just like you."

"*Stuck* here?" said Logan. "Oh, I am not '*stuck*' here! I

want to be here! That's the problem, Penny: you don't get it. And you never will. This camp, these girls, everything: this actually means something to us. We haven't come here every summer for eight years and we don't count the days until we get back here just for the hell of it. We believe in this place. *I* believe in this place. This is *my* place. It's the only place I really feel at home. It's the only place I really feel like myself and not just Logan Worthe, Queen Bee of Lakefield Academy. But now, it's ruined. Because of you."

"If this place and these girls are so special to you, then I shouldn't be able to ruin what you've built in eight years in just eight hours. Did you ever think of that?"

"What are you, captain of the debate team or something?"

"Maybe."

"Does Lakefield even have a debate team?"

Penny nodded.

"Really? What else do we have?"

But before Penny could answer, Logan shook her head and started talking again.

"Never mind. I have an idea," said Logan. "I don't want you to be here. And you don't want you to be here."

"I thought we established this already?"

"Can it, Nerd-girl."

"That's not nice."

"Whatever. So basically, if your parents aren't going to

just let you come home, we're going to have to get you *sent* home."

"What?"

"We have to get you sent home, kicked out, booted from Fern Lake. We just have to find the right rule—or rules—for you to break. That way, you get to go home and do whatever creepy-dweeby-debate-team-whateverness that you want to do, and we can go on with the summer we have been planning since we were eight years old."

"Kicked out of camp?"

"What? Are you scared? Afraid it might ruin your perfect high school transcript?"

"Well, quite honestly, *yeah*!"

"I'm not talking about you murdering someone, Penny," said Logan. "Maiming would be sufficient."

"What?" Penny yelled.

"Do they even *have* humor over there in the dweeb quandrant of the caf where you sit or what? I'll tell you the rules. All you have to do is break them. Don't worry, we'll have you home by Visiting Day."

"I will not have a criminal record!" blurted Penny.

"You've been watching too much TV, Penny. Frankie says 'Relax.' Enjoy your few days of camp while you have them. I guess it's going to be a great summer for both of us, after all. I'm really glad we had this chat. Oh, and Penny, why don't we make this our little secret? I've been campaigning for that damn spirit award for eight years now, and this year, it's in the bag. Got it?"

"Okay," said Penny.

Logan shook Penny's hand.

"It's a deal then!" said Logan, who smiled and skipped off across campus.

What had Penny just agreed to? Maybe Logan would forget their little deal, but she didn't seem like the kind of girl who just forgets that sort of thing. Penny's parents had promised her she could go home on Visiting Day if she wasn't having fun, but could Penny really count on them fulfilling that promise? They sent her here in the first place! So maybe adhering to Logan's plan was for the best? If all things went according to Logan's plan, Penny would get to go home after all, maybe even before Visiting Day, if she was lucky! Penny shook the whole thing off and tried to gather herself, to take deep breaths, and to generally *not* cry. This was now officially worse than high school. At least in high school, she could go home at the end of the day.

Penny attempted her entrance into Bunk One for the second time. She opened the door and walked in. She was "announced" by the rusty door latch, which clanged behind her, alerting everyone to her presence more loudly than she would have liked. Penny Moore was no longer the invisible-every-camper that she had been eight hours ago. She was now "the new girl."

The Bunk One girls were in midhug with a pretty red-headed girl whom Penny hadn't seen on the bus. Her name must have been Missy because they were chanting it over and over again. But, thanks to the loud clanging of the ancient door latch, the girls stared at Penny in silence.

"Sorry," she said.

Penny wondered when the word *sorry* had taken the place of *hi* in her extensive SAT-enhanced vocabulary. Penny was, for all intents and purposes, apologizing for her existence. The girls must have been as confused as she was because they remained silent.

Penny looked around the room. There were eight beds: seven thin blue-and-white-striped mattresses on old, rusty cotlike single bed frames, and one—closest to the front door— that was already made up neatly with white sheets and a thick red blanket. Six mattresses had the contents of the girls' carry-on bags already emptied out on them, claiming their territory. The contents inevitably rolled to the center of the mattress, as they all seemed to dip in the middle like hammocks.

The one unclaimed mattress was closest to the back door of the bunk. Penny walked toward it while the girls watched her. The floorboards groaned as she moved. With each step closer, several mysterious stains on the mattress came into focus. *Yuck.* She put her bag on top. It creaked, as if it was just as unhappy to have her sleep on it as she was. She bent down and eyed her "bed." It was official: Penny Moore had eaten fruit roll-ups that were thicker than this mattress. As she continued to inspect it, Penny heard whispering. She turned around, only to see the girls staring directly at her. Willow stepped forward toward Penny. She put the palms of her hands together and did what could only be described as a half-bow.

"I'm Willow," she said. "Welcome to the Promised Land."

"Hi. I'm Penny."

"What's with the bowing crap?" asked Missy.

"It's Willow's new greeting. I think it has to do with that family trip she just took to Asia," said Tess.

"It's a show of respect," said Willow.

Gabby burped loudly and blew on Willow.

"Ewww! Have you been completely submerged in a sour creamery since last summer?"

"So much for respect!" said Gabby. "And get it straight, it's sour cream and onion."

"I'm sorry for that, Penny," said Willow. "There's a kind of, oh, how do you say, atrophying of manners at camp."

"What's she talking about?" asked Missy.

"I lost her at trophies," said Gabby.

"She's saying we revert to ten-year-olds and get super-gross when we get back to camp," said Jade.

"In the spirit of inclusion and togetherness, I would like to introduce you, Penny, to Jade, Gabby, Tess, and Missy," said Willow.

"My boyfriend drove me up," volunteered Missy.

She pulled a framed photo off the windowsill by her bed and thrust it at Penny.

"Isn't he cute?" she asked.

"He's wearing a helmet," said Penny.

She grabbed the photo back and looked at Penny disdainfully.

"But I can totally tell he's cute, I mean, under the helmet," Penny added.

"He's going to college. We're staying together. Forever."

"Okay, psycho," said Jade.

"Cuh-reeeeeeepy," said Tess.

"In certain cultures, it is believed that the same souls find each other in different lives," said Willow.

"Yeah, that's totally us," said Missy.

"Don't encourage her!" said Jade.

"Willow, I think you have officially busted the enlightenment-o-meter."

"Ugh, can we please stop talking about 'the boyfriend'!" said Gabby.

"But I miss him, you guys! I'm, like, so excited to be here, but I just don't know what I'm going to do without him in the fall when he goes to college!"

The door opened, and Logan walked in.

"And this is Logan. Whom you, kind of, already met," said Willow.

"Hi," said Penny.

"Oh, Penny! I know Penny! Penny and I go way back! Did you guys know that Penny goes to Lakefield? Won't it be *fun* to have someone else from my own school in the bunk?" Logan put her arm around Penny's shoulders and gave her a noogie. The girls were clearly confused by and suspicious of Logan's strange behavior.

"Hey," Penny said . . . again. *Wait, she just said "Hi," didn't she?*

A phone rang. Penny breathed a sigh of relief. Never before had the sound of a designer ring tone been so sweet.

"Oh my God, Missy! Turn your phone off! They'll confiscate it!" said Gabby.

"I thought I put it on vibrate! It might be my boyfriend!"

"Missy, you can't keep your phone on all summer, seriously, you will so regret it when the summer is over and you've spent the whole time pining away for your boyfriend!" said Tess.

"I left my BlackBerry at home," said Logan. "It's so liberating. I can actually feel my fingers for the first time since I got it!"

"I left my phone at home, too," said Tess.

All the girls nodded in agreement.

"But I can't *not* talk to him every day!"

"But that's the beauty of camp, Missy!" said Logan. "No

phones, no e-mails, no IMs . . . this is the last summer of our childhood, girls!"

The door creaked open, and an older girl with a pudgy face stuck her head in.

"Sis boom bah Bunk One rah!" she said.

Her voice was high, almost babylike, just on the cusp between genuinely sweet and suspiciously saccharine. It was both endearing and unsettling at the same time.

"Annie!"

The girls screamed and ran toward her, falling down on their knees, and literally bowing down to her.

"We're not worthy! We're not worthy!" they said in unison.

"We are so psyched you're our bunk counselor!" said Tess. "We requested you!"

"I am so excited to be back in Bunk One again!" said Annie. "I vowed to get back here, even though all my college friends are in Europe. There's no place I'd rather be than back at FLC . . . where I belong. It's like a dream come true!"

"You are our inspiration," said Tess.

"Annie, will you bring us pizza and soda late at night?"

"If you're nice to me," said Annie. She looked past the group, and directly at Penny. "And you must be Penny. You, little Miss Thing, are the first girl in this camp's hundred-year history to enter into Bunk One as a first-year."

"Hip hip hooray!" said Penny.

And there was that silence again.

"Not so much with the 'Hip hip hooray,' huh?" Penny asked.

"Not so much," said Logan.

"We have our own cheers here," said Annie. "Don't worry. You'll learn them. Everyone does." Annie scanned the room, ultimately honing in on Missy. "Missy, is that a cell phone in your pocket or are you just happy to see me?"

"Um, no. It's . . . a tampon!"

"Right answer! Ten points for Missy!" said Annie. "Just remember, I didn't see anything. And don't let me see it again, okay?"

"Aye aye, Captain," said Missy.

"When in doubt, always say it's a tampon," whispered Annie. "Or that you have your period. Menstruation is the way to get out of everything at camp, especially with the male counselors, because the whole topic makes them really uncomfortable. But I didn't give you the four-one-one on that." Annie winked at Penny.

And then the girls launched into song . . . again. Penny wondered how they always knew which cheer was next? It was as if they had the camp version of ESP or something.

"We love you, Annie, oh yes we do
We love you, Annie and we'll be true

When you're not with us, we're blue-oo-oo
Oh, Annie, we love you!"

"Compliments will get you everywhere, girls."

"So, Penny, are you psyched to be here?" asked Annie.

"Psyched might not be the word I would choose . . ."

"Wah-waaaaaaaaah!" yelled Gabby.

The loud and bizarre noises coming from the girls were alarming at best as they all started echoing Gabby's "wah-waaaaaaaah!" Penny wondered just what they were doing. Were they making fun of her? Was this some other bizarre cheer she would have to learn in order to even remotely fit in?

"Oh no! Are you guys still doing the 'Debbie Downer' thing?" asked Annie. "I was sure you would be over it by this summer."

"Well, we're really excited to be here because camp is our favorite place on earth and the only place we can still be our true selves outside of current debilitating social stereotypes and constructs and outlandish expectations of young girls and we've been looking forward to this summer for our entire lives . . . *BUT* it will all be over before we know it and then we'll never get our youth back," said Willow.

"Wah-waaaah!" they yelled.

"So, I guess the answer is: yes?" asked Annie.

"The answer is," said Jade.

"Wah-waaaaaaaaah!" they screamed.

"Sound the Bunk One alarm, Debbie Dowwwwner!!!" yelled Missy.

The girls were now officially speaking in code. Penny wondered if she would be there long enough to decipher it.

"Anyway, welcome, Penny," said Annie. "You're a brave girl entering into Bunk One. So, it's supposed to rain later, girls—"

"Wah-waaaah!"

"Okay! You guys have already hit critical mass on the annoying meter. Can we please tone down the Downer this summer?" asked Annie.

"Ding-ding!" said Gabby.

"What's 'ding-ding'?"

"Gabby's trying to make it the anti-Downer," said Logan. "Like the analogies in the SATs: *good* is to *bad* as *ding-ding* is to *wah-wah*. *¿Comprende?*"

"Well, Logan, now that you've really put it into terms she can understand, I'm sure it's *crystal*," said Jade.

"No talk about SATs in the promised land!" yelled Missy.

Gabby put her fingers in her ears and closed her eyes and hummed so as not to even hear the word *SAT*. Penny clutched her backpack even tighter. Inside it were her now contraband SAT word lists.

"I hereby declare that there will be no more talk of 'the

standardized test that shall not be named' . . . for the rest of the summer!"

"Sis boomedy hurrah, no more talk about the standardized test that shall not be named!"

"Okay . . . ding-ding, girls, I get it," said Annie. "As I was saying, it's going to rain tonight—hold the wah-wahs!—so don't forget to close the shutters before dinner so your beds aren't sopping wet when we get back."

The girls leaned over their beds and uncoiled the ropes from the cleats on the wall. The wooden shudders slammed shut against the frames and screen windows just as a bell rang over the camp loudspeaker.

"Chow bell!" they yelled.

They hugged again and then accompanied the bugle tune from the loudspeaker by singing:

"Come and get your chow, girls, come and get your chow.
Come and get your chow, girls . . ."

They seemed to be doing some kind of bizarre and completely un-self-conscious a-rhythmic dance in the middle of the bunk. Limbs were flying, nostrils were flaring, snorts and wah-wahs and other bizarre noises were coming from their heads. Even Annie—who was supposedly their bunk counselor—joined in wholeheartedly.

Now, it's not that Penny hadn't done similarly spastic

dances before, certainly she had. She had just never done them . . . in front of other people. And weren't these supposed to be the "cool" girls? If they were, then Penny wondered why were they full-on embracing such dorkiness? Even Logan was un-self-consciously flailing with the rest of them . . . until she caught Penny looking at her, at which point she promptly stopped and glared at Penny.

"What are you looking at, Penny?" asked Logan.

"Nothing."

"I'm sorry, are we not cool enough for you? Are you too much of a rebel with a cause?" asked Logan.

"I think it's *without* a cause," said Missy.

Logan rolled her eyes. "I know it's *Rebel Without a Cause*, Missy, I was making a point."

"Oh."

"What was the point?" asked Tess.

"Okay, girls!" said Annie. "You all know that we're at Table One this summer."

"Sis boomedy hoorah, Table One!" they yelled.

"Who's our other counselor for meals?" asked Missy.

"Do you guys remember Joe Water Ski from last summer?" asked Annie.

"Uh, yeah. Duh? I mean, he was super hot!" said Missy.

"Yeah, he's not here this summer," Annie said, giggling. "You girls are so easy to fake out. It's like taking candy from a baby!"

At which point, Annie opened her palm to Gabby, who was sucking a gobstopper in her peripheral vision.

"How did you even see that?" asked Gabby.

"I was a camper for eight years, remember?"

"But I just put it in! I haven't even gotten through the second layer yet!" said Gabby.

Annie didn't say anything. She just thrust her hand toward Gabby again. Gabby spit out the round, wet gobstopper, which was bright blue.

"Cooooooooool! It was red like thirty seconds ago, I swear!" said Gabby. "Check this out, you guys!"

"So, seriously, who's the other counselor, Annie?"

"Do you remember Joe Sailing?"

"Oh, my," said Willow. "Do we ever! He was an attractive young man."

"Gabby was so in love with him!" said Missy.

"I was SO not!"

"You frenched a pillow pretending it was him!" said Tess.

"I did not!"

"Gab, I have it on video," said Logan.

"Damn!"

"So, he's at our table?" asked Missy.

"You're kidding!" said Tess.

"We are the luckiest girls in the WORLD!" said Missy.

"FAKE OUT!" yelled Annie.

"Noooo!" they yelled.

"Seriously, Annie!"

"Okay, okay! It's Dirk Tennis," said Annie. "He's new. He's from Idaho. He's a bit of a wah-wah, but I have no doubt you guys will break him."

"He has no idea what he's gotten himself into," said Gabby.

"No idea," said Logan.

The girls rubbed their palms together and smiled crookedly. They then put their arms around one another and ran out of Bunk One toward the dining hall. Penny heard girls screaming as they saw one another outside. The door slammed behind them, and Penny was finally alone for the first time all day. She looked around the small wooden bunk. The ceiling was high and had crisscrossing rafters like an upside-down game of pickup sticks. Penny imagined that once upon a time, all the wood had been several shades lighter, but had turned dark over the years: the floors, the walls, the ceilings, even the "cubbies," which were labeled for each camper with construction paper signs. There was a half-inflated fuchsia blow-up "couch" in the center.

There was writing all over the walls: mostly girls' names and the dates they were in Bunk One. Penny found dates as recent as 2006 and as old as 1954. All the signatures dedicated themselves wholeheartedly to Fern Lake Camp. In addition to the "graffiti" found everywhere, there were also bunk plaques hung along the walls and rafters. Each plaque had a different theme. They were all brightly colored and listed the girls who lived in the bunk that summer, and, of course, declared their undying love for FLC.

Penny just could not fathom what all the hype was about. It was a wood cabin with a bunch of bare mattresses and girls of decidedly questionable moral fiber. Sure the lake and the grounds were pretty, but "the promised land"? *Come on.*

Penny wouldn't normally consider herself paranoid or untrusting per se, but she still didn't want to leave her bag (word lists for "the standardized test that shall not be named," and all) unattended on her bed. Penny walked across the bunk to the low wall that separated the cubbies from the bed area. All the cubbies were connected to one another . . . except for Penny's. Her cubby was smaller and stood alone as an in-her-face afterthought. *Great, they stuck me with the pariah cubby.*

"Wah-wah," Penny said to herself. Damn, it *was* contagious!

When Penny opened her cubby, something small and brown and alive and rodentlike jumped out at her, bounced off her white camp uniform shirt, fell to the floor, and scurried away. *There are mice in "the promised land"?* Penny yelped and shut the door quickly.

Okay. That did not just happen. Fake out! she said to herself. Penny didn't even really know what a fake out was, but it seemed to be an appropriate response.

She shook her head. The last thing she wanted was to go into the lions' den that would be the dining hall. But she was hungry, so she took her knapsack with her to get her "chow."

CAMP RULE #5

Fern Lake ladies always
respect authority.

As Penny stepped out of Bunk One, she watched
girls in their pristine white and navy uniforms race from
all different parts of the campus toward the dining hall.
Some girls were more tentative, still wiping away fresh
tears. Other girls were running full speed toward the head
of campus with big, expectant smiles on their faces. Penny
realized that no one (aside from her) had a backpack with
them. She almost went back into the bunk to take it off, but
then she reminded herself that she was no Stepford camper!
She would wear her backpack to a meal if she wanted to.
Besides, Penny was supposed to be the kind of girl who dis-
obeyed rules and got kicked out of camp. Wasn't she?

The other campers looked at Penny with what she could
have sworn was reverence as they saw her stepping out of
Bunk One. When she returned their gaze, they turned away

immediately, as if staring someone from Bunk One in the eye would turn them to stone.

While she could hear the noise coming from behind the dining hall's screen doors, outside it was serene and quiet. Penny looked up to see ominously dark clouds looming above her, and she could feel the first few drops of rain falling on her head and hands.

Penny took a deep breath and walked up four steps coated in green AstroTurf. She opened the screen door to the sounds of dishes falling, utensils scraping against plastic, benches being pushed backward and forward on the linoleum floor, stomping feet, not to mention the irrepressible screams, cheers, and general excited chattering among the campers and counselors.

The dining hall had a high wooden ceiling and was enclosed by screened windows. It was about ten degrees hotter there than it was outside. The entire area was cooled only by a huge (yet ultimately useless, as it made more noise than cool air) fan. But no one seemed to notice or mind the heat . . . or the smell. To Penny, it smelled like one part spoiled tomato sauce, one part damp dog, and one part completely indiscernible quasifood.

There were girls lined up at two identical salad bars down the front center aisle of the dining hall. And then there were about thirty long rectangular Formica tables filled with girls sitting on the long sides, and counselors sitting at each end.

Campers were laughing, whispering, cheering, spilling bug juice, almost oblivious to or simply enjoying the noise and chaos. Penny scanned the crowded room for Bunk One. Instead, she spotted Morgan, whose arm was waving emphatically from the middle of the cafeteria. Penny waved back and watched as Morgan pointed Penny out to her bunkmates, accidentally stabbing one of them with her pointed index finger. Nevertheless, they all started waving. Penny smiled. *Maybe she could go sit with them.*

But then she saw it: the Bunk One table. The girls were together (of course), huddled at a table closest to the kitchen. In any restaurant, this would be the worst table. But at camp, Penny guessed, this was the coveted Table One. Penny ducked behind the chickpeas container at the salad bar before any of them could see her. She watched as Bunk One stood, put their left hands up while their right index fingers went to their lips, and they shushed everyone loudly, until a hush fell over the dining hall.

Penny held her breath and tried to be "the lizard" again, hoping to blend in to the chickpeas and be unnoticed. *Distress!*

Annie—and a serious-looking male counselor who must have been Dirk Tennis—had remained seated at either end of the table. Annie's head was down, but Penny could see that the ex-camper mouthed the words along with Bunk One as they said in unison:

"Let's all sing,
We're glad to see you back,
To . . . US!"

They started clapping as the rest of the campers (and Annie) cheered, laughed, and sang along in their loudest voices:

"Weeeeeeeeeeeeeeeeeeeeee're glad to see you back,
We're glad to see you back,
You know we are glad to see you back!
Yay, US!"

There was some more hooting and hollering and then the girls sat down again. Penny approached them tentatively. *Be the lizard*, she repeated to herself. Now, Penny Moore was totally accustomed to being ignored by the cool girls (namely, Logan Worthe). But it wasn't as if she didn't have friends. She just wasn't at "that" table in the caf. And now she was. Or at the very least, she was *assigned* to be there.

As far as Penny could tell at first glance, meals at camp were all about the condiments. In the center of the table were jars of mustard, ketchup, peanut butter, strawberry jelly, and grape jelly. It was comforting for Penny to see this, as she was pretty sure that if push came to shove food-wise, she could make a meal out of just these ingredients. Penny wouldn't starve. *Hurray*! she thought. *Or Sis boom bah! Or, whatever.*

The girls were so utterly ensconced in eating and cheering, that it wasn't until Penny actually hovered next to Annie that anyone noticed her.

"Oh, Penny! I was wondering when you were going to get here," said Annie.

"Sorry I'm late."

The girls stared at Penny blankly (except for Logan, who looked at her with genuine and undeniable contempt). Penny looked away and shoved her right hand into her shorts pocket.

"Logan, be nice," said Willow.

"Oh, pleeeease, Willow. Nice is my middle name!" said Logan.

"I thought it was Beth?" asked Gabby.

"Gabby, wake up and smell the sarcasm, would you please?"

"I'd rather smell the sarcasm than the food!" said Jade.

"Okay, move down, girls," said Logan. "I want my 'little sis' to sit next to me."

A dark shadow passed over Logan's face, leaving behind

a creepy super-size Mc-smile. Willow, who was sitting on one side of Logan, moved over hesitantly. Logan tapped the empty space on the bench next to her.

"Come on. I won't bite," said Logan.

Penny wasn't so sure about that, but she decided to risk it. She stepped over the bench with one leg, clumsily trying to climb into the narrow space in between Willow and Logan.

"You might want to take off your *backpack*," said Logan.

"Oh. Yeah," said Penny.

Logan rolled her eyes. With only one leg over the bench, Penny then awkwardly straddled it while she took off her backpack, almost hitting Logan in the process. It felt like a pickup game of Twister gone very, very wrong.

"Watch it, would you?" said Logan.

Penny put her backpack under the bench and then tried to slide closer to the table, but everyone had to stand up and push the heavy bench forward together. The bench dragged across the linoleum floor, making a noise that sounded distinctly like farting.

"Gabby, I told you, no more beans this summer!"

"That's so not funny, Jade!"

"Gabby has a bad stomach," explained Missy.

"I do not!"

"Okay, should we just say you are touched with 'the gas'?" asked Logan.

"I am not touched with 'the gas'! I have irritable bowel syndrome!"

"IBS is a myth," said Jade.

"No, it's not! IBS is real. It's a syndrome. And I have it."

While the girls bickered, Penny watched Annie just staring at a platter of so-called food.

"Does anyone want . . . I . . . I'm sorry, I have no idea what this is," said Annie.

"Don't knock it 'til you try it, girls," said Dirk Tennis. "That's lesson *numero uno*. Now, be a sweetheart and pass that bad boy down, would you?"

"Sure, *sweetheart*," said Annie.

Dirk dumped the gray meat onto his plate and literally shoveled it into his mouth . . . while he was still holding the tray! He had blond hair and blue eyes, and was exceedingly clean-cut. If he wasn't such an obvious jerk, Penny could see how someone might conceivably find him handsome. He sat up straight, like iron-pole-in-his-spine (though up-his-butt might be more accurate) straight. Penny must have been staring because he looked right at her and said with a gray-meat-mouthful, "It's not polite to stare."

Logan elbowed Penny. "Talk back to him," she whispered.

Penny mustered all her courage. "But talking with a mouthful of gray meat is?" she asked.

The girls were silent . . . until their silence turned into nervous laughter. Penny could tell they were surprised by her response to Dirk Tennis. But no one was more surprised than Penny herself!

Their nervous laughter then evolved into suspicious giggling and whispering. They shushed everyone in the dining hall again.

"Sound the Penny Moore alaaarm," they yelled. "Dirk Tennnnnnnnnnnnis!!!"

And that was how Penny, the newly appointed rule breaker of the group, almost died of embarrassment during the first meal of her sleepaway camp experience. Girls at other tables were staring at her. Counselors were staring. She contemplated running out. She contemplated crying. Or yelling. Or stomping her feet the way she used to do when she was three. Well, Penny reasoned, Logan did say summer camp was about reclaiming her youth, didn't she?

But before Penny could go anywhere, she was passed the platter full of gray mystery meat just as the girls broke into song . . . again.

> *"I like bananas, monkeys, nuts, and grapes,*
> *I like bananas, monkeys, nuts, and grapes,*
> *I like bananas, monkeys, nuts, and grapes,*
> *And that's why they call me . . ."*

The girls sitting across from Penny stood up, pounded on their chests, and yelled:

"Tarzan of the apes!"

As they sat down, all the girls on Penny's side of the table stood and did the same thing:

"Tarzan of the apes!"

Penny stayed seated as they did this again and again and again, until finally, on her way down from pounding her chest and laughing her heart out, Logan's elbow hit the corner of the gray meat tray. It toppled over (gray blood-juice that it was swimming in and all) right onto Penny's chest and lap. It was lukewarm, and wet, and super-processed, and just generally gross and gray.

"Oh my God! I am *so* sorry!" said Logan.

But considering she was in midlaugh, Penny had a feeling that Logan was not sorry at all. Jade turned away as her chest heaved and she was biting her lip and doing her best to hold in her laughter. Even the girls who Penny thought had seemed harmless and nice, like Tess, Missy, and Willow, put their heads down and pursed their lips to keep from laughing.

Penny felt her chin quivering. *No. Not going to cry. Deep breaths. Ding ding!* But it was getting worse. Penny's eyes were welling up. She tried to think of happy things like puppies and kittens, but then she remembered she loathed cats, and that kittens grow up to be cats and it's just a vicious cycle . . . so she kept thinking about puppies and happiness. *Please don't start crying*, she begged herself.

"Excuse me," she said.

Penny tried to climb out of her seat, but as she stood, pieces of gray meat stuck to her and gray juice rolled off her formerly white uniform shirt (which really should just have been a cool pair of Seven jeans!), and it must have made everything slippery because she toppled over the bench and fell on the ground behind it.

"Penny! Are you okay?"

Annie was immediately by her side, trying to help her up. But Penny couldn't even look her in the eye. If she looked Annie in the eye, she would have started to cry. She grabbed her backpack from under the bench and ran out the front door of the dining hall, leaving a trail of gray carnage in her wake. As the screen door slammed behind her, she heard laughter coming from Table One.

It had started raining outside—pouring, actually—and Penny was soaked by the time she reached Bunk One, even though it was only a good twenty feet from the dining hall to the bunk's front door. She slammed the door behind her and leaned against it as the rain dripped down her forehead and into her eyes. She looked around the room, which was suddenly spinning. Penny felt dizzy. Was it because she hadn't eaten since the gummy bears that Morgan had shared with her on the plane? Was it because she was drenched with rain and gray mystery meat juice? Was it because she just could not imagine living in this place for the next seven and a half weeks? Or D, all of the above? *D, definitely D,* thought Penny. Oh wait, was that a reference to "the standardized test that shall not be named"? Had she broken another cardinal Bunk One "rule" by even *thinking* multiple choice? Did Penny want to be a rule breaker? One thing was for sure: she knew she didn't want to stay in this strange place with these mean girls all summer. So, if breaking the rules was Penny's only way out, well, Penny Moore was going to break some rules.

Penny went over to her "bed" as the thunder crashed outside. And then she realized: she had forgotten to close her shutter. Her bare mattress was soaked through (all three cushy inches of it), and there was a pool of water around her bed. Perhaps she could have built an ark and floated home? Except Penny didn't think she would take one (much less two) of anything or anyone with her if she did.

Penny went into the bathroom just outside the back door of the bunk and locked the latch behind her. Everything was wood. It was like, you couldn't *not* get a splinter.

Luckily, the toilet was porcelain. So there was that. Penny put the lid down on the toilet seat, and sat on top of it, her clothes clinging to her like a wet T-shirt contest gone awry (especially considering the lack of boobage on her part). Penny looked around the old bathroom at the sink and the tiny, foggy excuse for a mirror above it, and at the square white cubbyholes on the wall. She realized at that moment that she hadn't seen any mirrors at all in the bunk. Weird. Maybe they were all vampires? Or, more aptly, "campires"?

Penny took a breath, which evolved into some variety of hiccups, and then she just started sobbing as quietly as she could. She put her face in her hands. Her eyelashes tickled her palms. Penny never thought of herself as one of those girls who constantly hostessed her own pity party, but at that moment, she felt really, really, *really* pitiful. She felt as if she had been taken captive by some bizarre tribe that spoke (or sang) a language she had never heard before. She couldn't help it if she wasn't fluent in "Cheerese!" The whole camp thing just didn't make any logical sense to her. Here were all these clearly privileged and rich girls spending a ridiculous amount of money every summer to come to Maine to a crappy little cabin with institutional mattresses, no mirrors, no Internet, and indiscernible/inedible food. Why would anyone keep coming back by choice—especially these girls? And what made them so fanatic about it?

Would Penny find out . . . before she was kicked out?

CAMP RULE #6

Fern Lake ladies are not slutty.

From the bathroom, Penny could hear the front door of the bunk creaking open and clanging shut several times as the girls returned from dinner. She heard them laughing, talking, unpacking, and moving beds (closer to one another and farther from her?). She was going to use her shirt to wipe the tears from her face but then realized it was still wet, so she used the palms of her hands, and then stood up and looked closely into the mirror. It was so old and foggy, she could barely see herself. But she saw enough to know that she was not looking her best. She certainly didn't feel it. *Wah-wah.*

Penny walked to the back door of the bunk and arrived just in time to hear Logan singing "Stayin' Alive." Penny peeked through the open door and saw the other girls unpacking while dancing around Logan. Missy, clearly the exhibitionist of the group, was wearing just her camp

T-shirt and boy-shorts-style underwear. She was pretending to "freak" the wall.

"Missy, could you be any sluttier?"

"Gabby! Don't judge! We're in the promised land!"

"Thank you, Willow," said Missy. "I'm just expressing myself . . . through dance."

"Okay, Slutty."

"I am not slutty! I am in a monotonous relationship!"

The girls laughed.

"What? What'd I say?" asked Missy in midshimmy.

"You're not slutty because you're in a boring relationship?" asked Jade.

"Missy, the girls are laughing because you misused a word and made an unintentional 'funny' in the process," explained Willow. "*Monotonous* means boring. But your relationship isn't boring, is it?"

Missy shook her head.

"Exactly," said Willow. "So you meant to say you're in a monogamous relationship, which means you are not seeing other people. It was a simple mistake."

"Willow, you're the only person I know who handles a simple word confusion like the Cuban missile crisis," said Logan.

"Who's having a missile crisis?" asked Gabby. "Wait a second, is that another bowel movement joke?"

"All I know is, I'm not slutty!" said Missy.

"It's a compliment," said Jade.

"It is?"

"Totally," said Tess.

"Okay. Then I guess you can call me slutty."

"We can all be slutty!"

"Cool!"

"Can one *be* slutty at an all-girls camp?"

"*Slutty* is just a word," said Willow. "For our purposes, slutty can mean whatever we want it to mean."

Gabby dramatically fell onto the inflatable couch, which made a farting noise as it started to audibly and visibly deflate.

"Not again, Gabby!"

"It was the couch! I swear!"

"First it was the bench, now it's the couch . . . ," said Jade.

"You guys, it's not funny! Don't be slutty! I'm having a missile crisis! Why does this always happen to me?"

"Wah-waaaaaah!"

"No, I'm serious. I've gained a lot of weight since last summer."

"Gabby, we're in the promised land. Earthly trivialities like calories don't exist in this alternate dimension," said Willow.

"Besides, you gained it all in your boobs," said Missy.

"Tell my butt that, slutmaster."

"You guys, what are we going to do about Penny?" asked Jade.

"Maybe she'll end up being slutty like us?" asked Gabby.

Penny was wondering how the word *slutty* had somehow become the acceptable substitute for all other adjectives.

"She seems slutty enough," said Tess.

"It's taken care of," said Logan.

"What do you mean, 'it's taken care of,' Lo-Wo?"

"Yeah, why so cryptic?"

"Nothing. Just a little cosmic equality, etc."

"Logan, what do you know about cosmic equality?" asked Willow.

"You're not the only 'enlightened' Fern Lake lady in Bunk One!" said Logan.

"Did you see the way she talked back to Dirk the Jerk?" asked Gabby. "She's got a little edge on her!"

"It wasn't that cool. I could have said it," said Logan.

"Logan, what's with the agro?"

"I'm always agro! This should be of no surprise to any of you!"

"Ooo, look at Lo-Wo's sheets!"

"Egyptian cotton. They're like four zillion thread count. I didn't have time to have them monogrammed unfortunately."

"Way to rough it, Lo-Wo."

"I got my older sister's hand-me-down Laura Ashley sheets from three seasons ago!"

"My mom got me Calvin Klein sheets, but they were 'irregular' or something so she got them half-price," said Gabby.

Penny had brought her old sheets from home. She wasn't sure they even had a thread count. She leaned closer to the door. Unfortunately, she didn't notice when it started to open until she looked up to see Gabby standing in the doorway, staring right at her.

"Oh, sorry," said Gabby. "I didn't know you were . . . there."

Penny mumbled something that even she couldn't quite decipher. Gabby closed the door behind her and walked past Penny toward the bathroom. But before she entered, Gabby turned around to face her.

"I know this must all seem weird to you now," said Gabby. "But it's really a slutty, I mean, a special place. And I don't mean that in a 'retarded' special kind of way. I mean that in a 'special' special way. Don't mind Logan. She's not so bad. She's just . . . a little high-strung."

"Oh my God! Did Cislyn forget to pack my neck pillow?! Oh, no!" yelled Logan from the other side of the flimsy wooden door.

"A little?" asked Penny.

"Cheer up, buttercup," said Gabby. "It's like day camp . . . only you spend the night, too."

"I never went to day camp."

"Oh. Well . . . then this is going to be nothing like anything you've ever experienced."

Suddenly, the door was flung open once again and Jade barreled through, pushing Penny and Gabby over in the process.

"Science experiment coming through, look out!" said Jade.

"Ow! Jade!"

"Gabby!"

"Watch where you're going! You nearly killed me!"

"Exaggerate much?"

"What's the science experiment?" asked Gabby.

"I'm fermenting grape juice. I'm hoping that by mid-July we'll have a viable water bottle full of wine. If anybody asks, it's raspberry Crystal Light."

"Got it."

Jade looked directly at Penny.

"You're not gonna be a snitch, are you, Moore?"

"I love Crystal Light."

"Good girl."

"Calling all campers," a voice declared over the loud-speaker. "All campers please report now to UTC."

"What's a UTC?" Penny asked, following the girls back into the bunk.

Penny was wondering why everything was abbreviated and if she would ever learn what anything meant . . . and, did she really care?

But none of them answered. The girls were too busy pulling on their sweats. Penny noticed that they had Bunk One stenciled on the backs of their hooded sweatshirts and down their sweatpants legs. Each camper's last name was written across the butt of her sweatpants.

"Sorry, Penny, my dad made these for us," said Gabby. "I didn't know you were going to be in our bunk so we didn't make one for you."

"Gabby's dad is a garmento!" said Missy.

"He owns sweatshops," said Jade.

"These were made in sweatshops?!" yelled Willow. She threw it on the bed like it was a poisonous snake.

"He does not own sweatshops! He makes 'affordable' clothes at 'affordable' prices."

Jade pretended to cough but she clearly said, "Sweat-shops!"

"Jade, that's like saying your dad is a butt doctor," said Gabby.

"Well, he is," said Jade. "He's a proctologist."

"Gross."

"Whatever," moaned Gabby. She painstakingly pulled the sweatpants up over her butt. "I had to get all new uniforms this year. It was so depressing."

"We're growing girls," said Willow. "It's only natural that our bodies should change."

"Gabby eats her feelings," whispered Missy.

"Eat *me*, Missy," said Gabby.

"See?"

"I do not eat my feelings! I just love food."

The girls slipped into their sweats, carefully rolling the tops of the pants down so that they landed just below their hips. After several digital pictures and some dancing in front of their bunk for all the younger campers to watch in awe, they headed over to UTC.

Penny was relieved when Annie spotted her from the counselor lounge and ran out to walk with her. Annie explained that UTC stood for "Under The Ceiling." Apparently, it was where the camp congregated most evenings, where plays and talent shows and just about everything else were performed. It was called Under The Ceiling because when the camp was started almost a hundred years before, the girls slept in tents. UTC was the only actual structure— the only real "ceiling" to be under.

Wearing her own plain navy blue sweatpants and white/gray-meat-juiced FLC uniform T-shirt, Penny followed the rest of Bunk One—in matching sweats and long johns tops and super flashlights and UGG boots—as they walked arm in arm.

Annie was Penny's tour guide, pointing out the new "lodge," which housed the camp offices (and the only place at camp that was actually air-conditioned). At the top of the hill, there were several green Adirondack chairs arranged in clusters under three huge elm trees. The chairs faced toward the rest of the camp: the long green grassy hill up to the campus from the waterfront with its own little beach. In between, there were tennis courts, basketball courts, several other buildings, and a barn with horses. There were sailboats on the beach, a huge pagoda over blue and white swimming lanes, and a floating dock alongside other open areas for swimming. On the grass just above the beach were rows of canoes and kayaks, and beyond them were three water ski boats at the dock. The girls stopped under the trees and sat in the Adirondack chairs for a minute just to admire the view.

"Look how beautiful everything looks!" said Tess.

"It's even more beautiful than I remember!" said Willow.

"But don't you think everything looks smaller?" asked Gabby. "I mean, remember how enormous everything was when we were juniors?"

"Wah-wah," said Tess.

"What? I'm serious! That's not a wah-wah, that's an observation. I can be very astute when I want to be," said Gabby.

"No, she's right . . . everything does look smaller, but the lake actually looks bigger than I remember," said Missy.

"Maybe it's retaining water?" asked Logan.

"Solid joke, Worthe," said Jade.

"Hey, Logan, the Catskills called. They want their punch line back," said Gabby.

Logan licked her index finger and made a hissing sound as she touched her own arm with it.

UTC came into view directly along their paved path. Penny followed the girls into the large log cabin. Inside, there were three sets of wooden bleachers, where most of the campers already sat. But one section of bleachers—the V.I.C. (Very Important Camper) section—was empty.

Penny watched as the other campers sat up and craned their necks to see the Bunk One girls make their entrance. She felt like she was part of a movie star's entourage (or in this case, of six movie stars). The girls climbed, one by one, through the lower tiers of bleachers where the younger campers were already sitting. The Bunk One girls put their hands on the younger girls' heads as they maneuvered their way up to the two tippy-top rows. Once there, the girls from Bunk One who sat in the second-to-top row leaned back in between the legs of the girls in the top row. Tess leaned into Logan, who kissed her head, squeezed her hand, and then clapped in front of her face while she swayed Tess's whole body with her knees to the beat of the song they were singing. Gabby leaned back in between Willow's legs, and Willow started to braid her long, straight—when painstakingly blow-dried—brunette hair. Jade leaned back into Missy—putting her arms on Missy's knees—as she looked over the camp like she owned it. And that left Penny, the odd camper out again.

"She shouldn't be allowed to sit here," whispered Logan. "I've waited my whole life to sit on these top bleachers."

"Let's see if she has the balls," said Jade.

The way Penny saw it, if Logan wanted her to be a rule breaker, then so be it: she would sit where she wanted to. So she made her way up the bleachers until she was on the edge of the top row.

"Hey," said Penny, mustering all her courage to sound ultracasual.

"I guess she does," whispered Jade. "Bully for her."

The other girls leaned forward and turned around to catch a glimpse of Penny. But before they could respond to her daring move, Stacy walked toward them from her chair by the side of the stage. She whispered to Logan and Missy, who then jumped down off the bleachers and proudly walked toward the stage. The head counselors and owners sat to the side in actual chairs. Penny never thought she would be envious of having a chair. As far as she could tell, camp was all about the benches (for the campers, anyway). Even Paxton got to sit in a small chair next to the adults.

He was wearing plastic sunglasses, and he whistled when Missy and Logan passed him.

"Looking good, girls," he said.

"Paxton!" yelled George.

"What's the problem, Daddy-O?"

"Just . . . take off your sunglasses," said Barbara.

"My future's so bright, I gotta wear shades, Barbara."

"I'm your mother."

"Cool."

On the other side of the stage was a wooden piano. Logan and Missy stood in the middle of UTC. Logan, the born politician, smiled warmly at the junior girls, who were sitting at her feet.

Then, in unison with Missy, she started to "song-lead." Penny watched Logan do the strange song-leading arm movement flawlessly and rhythmically. She started with her right arm bent, her right hand at her right shoulder. Her hand made a circle at her shoulder, and then she extended her arm, then bent it so that her forearm went across her chest, then back up to her right shoulder where her hand started the circle again. The movement continued, pacing the songs that the girls were singing. Every girl seemed to know the lyrics (and sometimes, even the harmony) to the songs. For Penny, it felt like a test for which she had not been given the right notes. Or any notes at all.

Penny scanned UTC. Girls of every shape and size from eight to sixteen were watching Logan and Missy attentively, singing heartily with smiles on their faces. They were all touching one another in some way, leaning back into one another's laps, arms around one another, hands in one another's hair. They whispered at moments, giggled, but ultimately, they were singing as one happy three-hundred-headed camp monster.

Penny could sense that the girl hierarchy was already being established in every age group. The girls who were crying quietly stuck together, while the girls who brazenly mouthed the words of the songs they did not yet know would end up leading their bunks, their age groups, and eventually, the camp. As Penny saw it, the lyric-mouthers were the Logans. The ones with their blankies and stuffed animals and puffy eyes, well, that would have been . . . Penny. Or would it? Was it ever too late to be a lyric-mouther? And where did the rule breaker fit in, if at all?

Penny noticed Morgan sitting on the floor. She was still wearing her eye patch, but her tears—from the left eye, at least—had dried up, and she was self-consciously mouthing the words to the songs. She turned around and waved vigorously at Penny, accidentally knocking out the camper sitting next to her.

Logan and Missy hugged Barb and George on the way

back to their seats. Barb and George welcomed all the girls to a new Fern Lake Camp summer. At which point, Bunk One started clapping and singing:

"Barb and George,
Their greatness you can't forge.
George loves his socks,
Barb has blond locks.
We love you both,
You are the most!!!
Sis boomedy hoorah, Barb. Sis boomedy hoorah, George.

Sis boomedy hoorah, socks!"

According to Barb and George, the first night of camp every summer included their tag-team reading of the annually evolving Fern Lake Camp story. They took turns reading from an old journal that described the camp's history, which started in 1910 when the headmistress of a school in New York City brought several girls to Maine for the summer. She bought a piece of property with only one structure built on it. That structure was right where they were all sitting: Under The Ceiling. As time went on, several beloved FLC owners came and went, more buildings were built bearing their names, more songs were written and added to the ever-growing Fern Lake songbook, but all the old traditions remained the same, and new traditions evolved. Penny thought it was kind of a cool story. Unfortunately, it only added to her confusion about what she was missing with this whole camp thing. What was it about this place that had endeared so many girls to it for a century?

As they left UTC, most of the girls were still arm in arm. Penny followed them straight to the flagpole, where all three hundred campers held hands (right arm over left arm), and the Bunk One girls, in the center of the circle, led the singing. Penny had not yet learned how to song-lead and clearly did not know any songs, so she slinked away from the flagpole and joined the rest of the campers in the more anonymous main circle. Apparently, this would be done again the night of Visiting Day, and on the very last night of camp. Between the bright stars overhead, and the moving spotlights coming from the song-leaders' flashlights, the moment felt eerily important, even though Penny knew she shouldn't care.

When the girls got back to the bunk, Penny decided to put her sleeping bag on the floor because her mattress-roll-up was still soaked. She changed into her Hello Kitty night-gownshirt in the bathroom while all the other girls just stripped down nonchalantly in the middle of the bunk. Penny was a little self-conscious that way (especially around girls who she was pretty sure hated her). It was only a short walk from the bathroom to her mattress-roll-up, but it was just long enough for Logan to spot Penny slipping into her sleeping bag.

"*Hello Kitty?*" Logan screeched. "Hey, everybody, 1998 called, they want their nightgown back!"

"I totally had that nightgown when I was eight!" said Gabby. "It was my favorite."

"Yeah, that's when I got this, too," admitted Penny.

"Ooh, vintage!" said Logan, sarcastically.

"Yeah, except I could never fit into mine anymore," said Gabby.

"WAH-WAH!"

They started hitting Gabby over the head with their pillows.

"I think it's very retro," proclaimed Willow. "You know, Hello Kitty revolutionized the whole Japanese anime movement."

"Thanks," said Penny.

Thanks? As the lights went out across campus, Penny hit herself on the head for answering Willow so stupidly. *No wonder they don't like me,* she thought.

"Spooooooooky!" the girls cried in the darkness.

"I am the slutty ghost of Fern Lake!" said Gabby, her flashlight under her chin.

Penny closed her eyes and imagined being home in her own bed. She pawed her nightgownshirt and sniffed it deeply, welcoming the comforting smells of her mother's preferred detergent. She started to wonder how she might have fared at camp as an eight-year-old. If she was sixteen and this homesick, how homesick would she have been at the tender age of eight? Maybe she just wouldn't have known any better? Either way, Penny was exhausted and hungry. And then she remembered! She had a piece of sour apple Hubba Bubba in her backpack. She reached out and dragged her bag toward her from under her bed, and dug out the stray piece of gum. There were bits of unidentifiable lint stuck to it, so she wrapped it up and put it back in her bag. *Wah-wah, indeed.*

CAMP RULE #7

Fern Lake ladies always
complete their required
swimming rectangles.

The following morning, Penny Moore woke up to a very loud bugle noise blowing directly into her ear. Okay, maybe it wasn't blowing *directly* into her ear. Maybe it was playing over the loudspeaker. It was definitely playing over the loudspeaker. She sat straight up and felt a shooting pain in her neck from sleeping on the floor all night. A couple of the girls groaned, which quickly morphed into groggy cheers.

"Reveille!" said Missy. "I can't believe I actually missed the sound of reveille!"

"I downloaded reveille to my iPod and had it wake me every morning during the school year," said Gabby.

"That is soooo slutty!" said Missy.

"Isn't it too early to be slutty?"

"It's never too early to be slutty."

"Super dork, to the rescue! Her theme song is reveille!" Jade yelled as she jumped out of her bed, using her blanket as a cape.

Gabby threw her pillow at Jade.

"Too early for pillow fights," said Logan. "Need coffee."

Bunk One threw on uniforms over their pajamas, and walked to breakfast. Penny followed. The rain had stopped, and the sun was fighting to peek through the clouds. The dining room looked even bigger in the daylight, and there was a cereal bar where the salad bar had been the previous evening. Bunk One climbed over the benches at their table and sat down. Penny sat at the end, with one butt cheek off the bench, while the other girls scrambled for coffee and blew on their mugs dramatically.

"Ah, lukewarm brown water. God, I missed this stuff," said Logan.

"Nine out of ten coffee drinkers agree that this is not actually coffee," said Jade.

"While these campers were not looking, we replaced their coffee with dishwater. Let's see if their young, discerning palates can tell the difference," whispered Logan. She held up her spoon to Willow, as if it were a microphone.

"It's like the essence of sunshine captured in a mug!" said Willow.

"Mmmm," said Jade. "It takes me back to those cozy mornings as a drug dealer in Colombia."

"It gives me that get up and go I need so desperately in the morning!" said Tess.

"The aroma is just . . . intoxicating. It's like . . . great sex," said Missy.

"Well, do I have news for you girls?!" said Logan. "You're on hidden camera! What you're actually drinking isn't coffee at all. It's dishwater!"

"I never would have known!" said Tess.

"*Bllllgh*," said Jade as she pretended to vomit under the table.

"But I'm not ready for my close-up!" shrieked Missy.

"That is so slutty!" said Gabby.

"Would you girls stop fooling around and pass the coffee already?" interrupted Dirk.

Bunk One had already changed Dirk's name to "Dirk the Jerk" (okay, it wasn't much of a leap, but if the nickname fit . . .), and the girls seemed to have it in for him. Penny kept quiet until breakfast was over and it was time to return to the bunks. They had forty-five minutes to get Bunk One ready for inspection. None of the girls had even finished unpacking . . . except Logan. When Penny opened her duffel, it smelled like home, and another wave of homesickness hit her. Whereas Penny wanted to curl up inside her duffel and send herself home in it immediately, the other girls felt the opposite.

"Out out, damn luggage!" said Willow.

"We need all remnants of the 'real' world out of sight!"

After piling the empty luggage into a corner and draping towels over it so that they wouldn't have to see it, the girls started arguing over who was supposed to clean what and when and why. Annie arrived just in time, holding what looked like an arts-and-crafts project gone awry.

"Good morning, girls!" said Annie. "This right here is your summer work wheel!"

Annie held up a circle of green paper fastened onto a larger tan piece. On the tan piece were the names of all the girls in the bunk. The green circle was divided up into seven chores.

"As an artistically challenged person, this project here took me about six days and about sixty trees' worth of construction paper to make, so please use it, girls," pleaded Annie. "If you don't do it for me, for God's sake, do it for the trees!"

"Hear, hear!" said Willow.

"Pipe down, hippie," said Jade.

"Jade, maybe we should discuss why you have a need to label people with such antiquated stereotypes," said Willow.

"Blow me," said Jade.

"Okay then!" said Annie. "The work wheel! Let 'er rip! Spin, spin, spin, spin . . ."

Annie chanted and the girls quickly joined in. They got

increasingly louder until they were yelling and jumping up and down. And then . . . silence.

"Did I forget to pick someone to spin the wheel?" asked Annie.

"Yup."

"Shoot!" said Annie. "Okay, that was exhausting. I'm just going to close my eyes and spin the wheel myself."

The wheel barely moved and the construction paper ripped a little.

"Love your work," said Jade.

"I'm going to pretend I didn't hear that," said Annie. "Okay, Logan and Willow: you've got a free day."

"Hooray!" they yelled.

"Jade and Tess: sweeping, Missy: dust-panning, Gabby: grounds, and Penny: greenie."

"What's a greenie?" asked Penny.

"That's what Fern Lake ladies lovingly call . . . the john," said Jade.

Talk about a wah-wah.

But Penny did not audibly complain. Instead, she went into the bathroom, which was already a mess. The cubbies were now overflowing with toiletries and expensive products. There was mud on the floor and dried toothpaste in the sink. Penny did her best to clean up, but as she was about to leave, Logan appeared in the doorway.

"So, let's go over today's rules and your subsequent breaking of said rules."

"Um, okay."

"You might want to skip assembly today," said Logan.

"Okay, why?"

"My new theory is that since you're probably not brave enough to do one big thing to get yourself kicked out, you'll have to do a bunch of small things that add up. So, let's start with not coming to assembly."

"Okay, I guess. I didn't want to come to assembly anyway," said Penny.

"I figured as much," said Logan. "Okay, so, cool. See you later. Oh, and Penny, you missed a spot."

Before Penny could think of some smart retort, chimes sounded over the loudspeaker, and all the girls yelled with excitement. They ran outside in their one-piece bathing suits with uniform shorts over them, and they linked arms. All campers stood in front of their bunks as the American flag was raised in the middle of campus. Then, Bunk One—with arms linked—ran toward the flagpole, singing the whole way. Bunk One, minus Penny, that was. Penny sat on Annie's bed and watched from behind the screen.

Penny felt lonely. And sad. And homesick. And most of all, she felt angry. She was angry with her parents for sending her there, angry with Logan for being so mean, and angry with herself for not being . . . cooler.

The younger girls followed from the other bunks and met Bunk One in the center of campus. The campers sat on the grass around the flagpole while Stacy made some scheduling announcements, and then dismissed assembly when she was done.

Penny followed after Bunk One as they walked down the rolling hill, past the tennis courts, to the waterfront, where they had first-period swim. Each girl put a little metal washer on individually name-tagged hooks and walked single file onto the dock under the pagoda. Missy pinched Gabby's butt.

"Cut it out, Slutty!" laughed Gabby.

"No messing around on my deck!"

A robust woman with a deep voice, short blond hair, and red cheeks appeared as if from nowhere, carrying her clipboard. She wore Tevas, a black Speedo one-piece bathing suit, and navy shorts—which were pulled up so far they might as well have been a turtleneck. She reeked of waterproof sunscreen and an obviously inflated sense of power.

"That's Sherry. She's head of swim. We call her C.T.," whispered Missy.

"Why C.T.?"

"Camel Toe," whispered Gabby.

"What do you expect when your shorts also function as a scarf?" asked Logan.

Penny couldn't help but laugh. Sherry glared at her and cleared her throat. Penny followed the other girls as they lined up on the dock in front of an open rectangular area, next to six neat swim lanes. After much pulling and snapping of plastic, the girls managed to put on their caps, most with pieces of hair awkwardly jutting out of them. Logan's cap—the only white one in a sea of color—fit perfectly. *Of course.* She wore the cap sideways so that the crease ran from the front of her head to the back, like a plastic Mohawk.

"Welcome back, ladies," said Sherry. "As you all know, the first day of camp is swimming rectangles. You can not do any water sports until you complete your required rectangles. I know it's your favorite."

"She must have been working on her sarcasm all year long. That's a new thing for her," whispered Jade.

"You know the drill. Drop and give me ten rectangles."

Missy raised her hand.

"And don't even think about using the 'it's that time of the month' excuse," said Sherry.

Missy slowly lowered her hand.

Logan was the first to jump in. When she came up for air, she was out of breath, clearly from the coldness of the water.

"Nothing like first-period swim!" Logan said with a forced grin on her face.

"Logan won the swim award last summer," said Willow. "And the field hockey award. And the pottery award."

"It's still unclear how she tackled that last one, considering no one ever saw her in the pottery shop," said Gabby.

"But no one puts anything past 'The Worthe,'" said Jade, who then casually pushed Willow into the water.

"Jade, you have major rage issues you really should deal with!" shrieked Willow.

"Can it, Willow," said Sherry. "Jade, you're in Bunk One now! You are supposed to be setting an example. What have I told you since you were a junior about not pushing on the waterfront?"

"Sorry, Sherry. I must have forgotten over the school year. Guess that means I'll have to sit out on the fun that is swimming rectangles, doesn't it?"

"You know that's not how it works. Not on my ship."

"Ship?" Penny whispered.

"She's a little maniacal about the waterfront," explained Tess.

"Ten hut, girls!" yelled Sherry.

"A little?" Penny asked.

"Jade, you just bought yourself ten extra rectangles."

"Thank you, sir, may I have another?" asked Jade.

"Don't be cute, Jade. It doesn't become you," said

Sherry. And then she looked over at Penny. "Who are you? Are you supposed to be here? This is Bunk One. Are you in Bunk One?"

"Yes, sir . . . I mean, ma'am. I'm new."

"Well, New, then I suppose you need to be tested for a bathing cap."

"Tested?"

"At Fern Lake Camp, we swim for form. Yes, we have swim meets and that's for speed, but we are known for our Fern Lake lady form. The colored caps illustrate what level you are. Logan is a white cap. That is the best."

Surprise, surprise.

Logan treaded water and glowed with pride. Or maybe it was the beginnings of hypothermia. It was hard to tell.

One by one, the girls jumped in. Jade took a step back from the edge and then ran and jumped off the dock into the water, doing a cannonball.

"No running! Jade Furlong, I'm watching you!" yelled Sherry.

Missy sat down on the side and slid in hesitantly, scratching her thigh in the process. She stuck her butt up out of the water midstroke and yelled, "Am I bleeding?"

"No, Missy, your butt is not bleeding," said Jade.

"I wonder, does exhibitionism run in your family?" asked Willow.

Gabby squeezed her nose tight with her fingers and

closed her eyes, as if preparing for a long and painful descent into the Arctic Sea. And Tess just dove straight in (with perfect form). This left Penny, capless and the only dry Bunk Oner. The girls had started swimming in rectangles, counting out loud each time they passed the ladder. Sherry gave Penny a brand-new orange cap.

"Orange cap: the lowest of the low. No special treatment here, Missy."

"What?" yelled Missy from the water.

"Not you, Missy, her-Missy."

"But her name's not Missy!"

"Don't be a smart-ass, keep swimming!"

"Did she just say something about my ass?"

"Listen, New," Sherry continued, "I don't kid myself into thinking that the girls from Bunk One will keep coming to swim after the first day. So just take this, and let's call it a day, shall we?"

Penny shrugged her shoulders, pulled her cap on, and dove into the lake. It was shockingly cold. She caught up with Gabby, who was also in an orange cap.

"When we were younger, passing a stroke and getting to the next cap was a big deal," said Gabby. "And the higher level you were, the more strokes you had to pass and the more perfect they had to be. I never really got into it."

"May I cut in?"

Logan had swum up in between Gabby and Penny.

"Swim with me, would you?" asked Logan.

Logan was a fast yet beautiful swimmer. Her freestyle stroke was perfect, effortless. Watching Logan Worthe swim was like watching a pedigree horse run a race.

"Hide under the dock," said Logan.

"Excuse me?"

"You need to disappear, freak them out."

"I need to breathe, is what I really need."

"There's room to breathe, dummy. Just go under the dock, and when you come up there's a good three inches of room in between the water and the underside."

"Sounds scary. And claustrophobic."

"Did you ever make a fort with pillows when you were a kid?"

"Yeah."

"Well, it's just like that."

"Except I'm not in my bed and there are no pillows."

"Exactly."

"And I'm under water, alone in the freezing cold darkness."

"Okay, it's *sort of* the same thing."

"I'm not so sure it's—"

"You want out of here, don't you?" asked Logan. "Think you can spend seven more weeks in this lake?"

The lake *was* quite cold. Logan increased her speed and swam off before Penny could answer. All the girls were chatting and bickering, and Sherry was flossing her teeth using the metal clip on her clipboard as her mirror. Penny saw her moment, veered off from the rectangle, and dove under the surface. When she came up for air, her forehead hit the bottom of the dock, which was covered in some bright green slime.

"Yuck!" she said, and then immediately covered her own mouth. Penny treaded water while she listened to the girls chatting. Clearly, no one had even noticed that she was gone.

"Jade, do you remember the year you came to camp with cornrows and you couldn't fit your hair underneath the cap?"

"I remember that she didn't wash her hair all summer to keep the cornrows intact and they started to reek," said Gabby.

"And then she got lice," said Tess.

"And gave it to everyone else!"

"The next summer was the mullet."

"I did not have a mullet!"

"You SO did."

"You say tomato—"

"And I say mullet."

"Business in the front, party in the back!" said Logan.

"This activity is called 'swim,' girls . . . it's not called 'talk'!" yelled Sherry.

Penny could hear that Sherry was walking along the

dock toward her. Unfortunately, when Penny looked up: she had a direct view of the infamous Camel Toe. Penny made a vow to never, *ever*, wear her shorts on her waist again.

And then, a loud whistle blew.

"Buddy up!" a deep male voice called.

"Mike Canoe!" yelled the girls.

"Mike Canoe!" said Sherry. "This is not your domain. Put down that whistle this instant!"

"Sherry, baby, I've been here for sixteen summers. Every domain is my domain. Plus, Bunk One never finishes their rectangles. It's an unspoken tradition. You should know that."

"Foiled . . . again!" said Sherry. "Wait a second. There are only six of you. Where's New?"

"What's new?" asked Mike Canoe.

"Not much," replied Sherry.

"What?"

"What?"

"Who or what is New?"

"Her name is Penny!" said Logan.

"Whatever. Where is she?"

Penny didn't hear anything from the girls. She was terrified. And then she heard multiple whistles blowing.

"Get the divers!" yelled Sherry.

"Sherry, we don't have divers," said Mike Canoe.

"Somebody find this camper!"

Okay, clearly the party was over. It was time for Penny to come out from under the dock and incur the wrath of Sherry, head of swim.

"It's okay! I'm okay!" Penny yelled from under the dock.

She took a deep breath and dove under the water. She swam under the surface until she could see the girls' legs treading water, and then came up inside the swimming rectangle next to them.

"New! What were you doing down there?"

"First of all, my name is not New. It's Penny. And I was just checking out your little swim area. There's a lot of gooey green stuff under the dock. You might want to think about getting it cleaned."

Sherry was in shock. The girls cracked up. Gabby gasped, her gum dropped out of her mouth, and she took in a mouthful of water. She started coughing. Sherry, seeing Gabby coughing, immediately blew her whistle again, threw down her clipboard, and jumped into the water, camel toe and all.

"Hang on, Gabby, I'm coming to get you!" yelled Sherry.

"But I'm fine," said Gabby. "I just swallowed a bit of water."

"That's what you say now, and then you drop to the bottom of the lake like a stone, and then suddenly you're just a statistic!"

"Was that a fat joke?"

"Statistic?"

"No, stone!"

Sherry reached Gabby and gruffly put one arm around her waist, swimming her to the ladder.

"I am fiiiiiiiiiiiine!" said Gabby.

"You're just lucky I was there in time. That was a close call. Another camper saved!" said Sherry. "Okay, everyone out of the water now. And, Penny New, I want you to report back here at rest hour the next five days. You think the deck is dirty, you're going to clean it. Bring your toothbrush."

The girls swam past Penny toward the ladder.

"Wow. Haaarsh," said Logan. "Good luck with that."

"Gee, thanks," said Penny.

"Rectangles are totally patriarchal anyway," whispered Willow.

"Way to take on C.T.," said Jade. She knuckle-punched Penny.

"That was *so* slutty! Way to go," said Missy.

Penny followed the girls up the ladder to the dock. Gabby, who was already wrapped in her purple towel, approached Penny.

"I go under the dock all the time to finish my Jolly Ranchers and other time-oriented sucking candies. Way to get right into the spirit of things!" said Gabby.

Penny couldn't help but smile. She had to admit: she kind of liked being the rebel, even if she was a rebel with a BE-cause: because she had no other choice.

CAMP RULE #8

Fern Lake ladies take only one
cookie at cookie line. Please.

I think I have water in my ear," complained Gabby.

She was still on the dock, hitting the side of her head with the palm of her hand. Jade walked past her and hit the opposite side of her head.

"Ow!" said Gabby.

"Just trying to help!" said Jade, and then she turned and giggled with Tess and Willow.

"What? Just trying what? I can't hear anything!" yelled Gabby.

Chimes rang over the loudspeaker.

"Oh! cookie line!" Gabby yelled.

"She heard that!" said Tess.

"Everyone hears cookie line," said Missy.

"Cookie line?" asked Penny.

"Nobody told you about cookie line?" asked Jade.

"That's usually the first thing people talk about! Every day at eleven-thirty A.M. just after first period, chimes ring to signal cookie line."

Jade's response didn't really answer Penny's question, but she nodded, as she had been doing incessantly since she got there. She followed the Bunk One girls as they walked back up the hill. Their wet bathing caps were in their hands and the fever for the flavor of a Fern Lake-cookie-line cookie was clearly in their hearts . . . and stomachs.

"Oh, I hope it's M&M cookies, I really really do!" said Gabby.

"Just as long as it's not peanut butter," said Missy.

"I know! Remember when we had to roll Willow to the infirmary the last time she had peanuts? I've never seen someone swell up like that," said Gabby.

"I'm not crazy about oatmeal raisin," said Logan. "I feel like it's too healthy. If I'm going to have a cookie, I'm going to do it right."

"Oh my God . . . chocolate chocolate chip!"

"I'm not supposed to have any," said Tess. She was staring at the laminated nutrition plan her tennis coach had made for her.

"Says who?" asked Jade.

"Coach Keller."

"Coach Keller sucks."

"Jade . . ."

"I mean, it's enough that you have to convince your parents every summer to let you come back here when they know how much it means to you. But it's ridiculous that they still try to control you when you're here."

Tess rolled her eyes as they walked past the swings underneath a cluster of trees. Penny's towel was falling off her waist, while Logan's towel was wrapped snugly around her own. Jade had her navy blue Umbro shorts over her wet bathing suit and put the towel around her neck, because, she said, that was how she "rolled." Gabby had the towel tied over her formidable chest. Missy was staring at it intently.

"Your cleavage is truly inspiring," said Missy.

"What?" asked Gabby. "I can't hear anything!"

The rest of the girls struggled with their various articles of clothing, towels, and other athletic accoutrements. Willow tucked her towel into the back of her one-piece bathing suit so that it looked like a cape.

"What are you, Super Hippie?" asked Jade.

"Don't be jealous, Jadey, just because I have an ecological conscience."

"Do you guys think I can call my boyfriend now?" asked Missy.

"I thought you got rid of your phone?" asked Gabby.

"I thought you had water in your ear?"

"What?" asked Gabby.

"Guys, we're going to miss cookie line . . . come on!" said Logan.

"We can *not* miss cookie line," said Gabby.

They started to run up the hill to the main house. There were other campers running from all directions to stand in the line that snaked up the old stone staircase onto the porch of the main house. Some of the younger girls on the line were pretending they were song-leaders (like the big girls), instructing one another and correcting one another's song-leading form. But as Bunk One approached, the girls stopped immediately and became silent. Without a word, the sea of girls parted and Bunk One (and Penny) walked right through all of them, going directly to the front of the line. The line led up to a table set with two plastic bins: one filled with fresh chocolate chip cookies, the other with orange wedges. A skinny old man in an FLC uniform stood like a security guard, regulating the cookies. When he opened his mouth to speak, the girls spoke right along with him.

"One cookie please!!!" They said in unison.

The cookie man was named Jon. Gabby told Penny that Jon always watched that cookie bin like a hawk. He had been working there forever (way before these girls were even juniors), summer in and summer out, standing guard over the famous Fern Lake cookies (regardless of flavor), and repeating the phrase "one cookie please." What was weird was that, apparently, no one saw Jon at any time other than cookie line. He and his cookie-hawk eyes appeared at eleven-thirty every morning like clockwork and then disappeared until cookie line the following day. And no one ever saw him actually eat a cookie. It was also unclear if he had any say in deciding that day's flavor, or had any part in baking them. Obviously, this had been a major topic of conversation among the girls on more than one occasion.

"Go for two cookies," whispered Logan.

"But I don't want two cookies," said Penny.

"We had a deal," said Logan.

Penny watched as the girls gleefully grabbed one cookie each and as many orange wedges as they could manage. They washed it all down with little plastic cups of ice cold milk (soy milk for Willow). Penny came up last, taking one cookie, which she dropped on the deck but picked right up again.

"Um, Jon, I'm sorry to bother you," said Penny. "But my cookie fell on the ground. May I please take another?"

Penny could see Logan staring at her and wagging her finger. "Cheater," Logan mouthed.

"One cookie, please," he said.

"But mine fell on the ground!" pleaded Penny.

"One cookie please," he said.

Penny shrugged, defeated. She wasn't about to grab a cookie and make a run for it. She looked up, and Logan held up two fingers and pointed to her eyes, as if to say "I'm watching you."

And then Penny felt a hand take hers. She looked up at Jon. He didn't even make eye contact, but he slipped Penny a second cookie. And without skipping a beat, he repeated "one cookie, please" to the next camper.

Penny clutched her two cookies and approached the girls, holding her plastic cup of milk with her teeth.

"Hey, Penny, did you get two cookies?" asked Missy.

"She's got TWO cookies!" said Gabby.

"Did you beat up a junior for it?" asked Jade.

"She just dropped her first one," said Logan. "It doesn't count."

"It so does count!" said Penny. "Two-second rule: I learned it from Gabby yesterday . . . on the bus."

"I am honored!" said Gabby.

Penny smiled as she took a huge bite of the controversial fallen cookie. "Anyone want another cookie?"

"Penny, you're my new personal hero!" said Gabby.

"No, you're mine!" said Penny.

Logan rolled her eyes. "Booooring!" she said.

"I'll have some, too," said Missy.

"Hand it over," said Jade.

"Oh my God! This is the best cookie I have ever had in my entire life," said Gabby. "Are you going to eat that cookie, Tess-ster?"

"Yeah, how's that orange wedge, Tessie?"

Tess smiled hugely, revealing just the orange rind instead of her teeth. "Great," she mumbled.

Logan put her arm around Tess's neck and kissed her on her head. Tess smiled her big orange smile. Willow was very busy inspecting her cookie and then nibbling it just around the edges.

"Hey, Carob Chip, what happened to your vegan diet?" asked Jade.

"If you must know, I happen to be eating around the chocolate chips," said Willow.

"It's still not vegan."

"I am aware of that, Jade, and I have made my peace with it, so if you could let me enjoy my cookie, I would really appreciate it."

"What do you think of your first Fern Lake cookie, Penny?" asked Missy.

Penny had just taken her second bite and was in the process of washing it down with a huge gulp of milk. She looked at her half-eaten cookie and then at the girls. She knew she shouldn't talk with her mouth full. But this was the first real question the girls had asked her, the first time they had actually engaged her in conversation. And now she had to respond with a mouthful of food.

"Ish gooo," she managed to say.

Unfortunately, in the process of trying to speak, Penny

spit out a big chunk of cookie right onto Logan's treasured white cap.

"Nice," said Logan.

The girls laughed. Disgusted, Logan kneeled down and wiped the cap on the grass.

"Great. And now it has grass stains!" said Logan.

"Wah-wah!" said Gabby.

Penny finally swallowed her mouthful.

"Sorry," said Penny.

"Who's going back to the bunk? I have to get my tennis racket," said Tess.

"I'll come with you," said Willow. "I have to start planting my garden."

"Could you plant some Sour Patch Kids? I love those," said Gabby.

"Gabby, you can't actually plant candy . . ."

"Willow, I know. It was a joke. I'm not that stupid, but thanks for the vote of confidence."

"I wasn't saying you were stupid!"

"Talk to the hand, Willow, talk to the hand."

"I have to go change my shirt . . . and disinfect my cap," said Logan. "And then maybe I'll go watch some of the junior activities."

"Who are the juniors?" asked Penny.

"Do we have to explain everything to you?" asked Logan.

"The juniors are the youngest age group. They're usually around eight years old. And then there are several age groups in between."

"We were seniors last year, and this year, we're . . ."

"Bunk One!" they yelled in unison.

"So, why would you be going to watch a junior game if they're only eight?"

"Because Logan is *totally* trying to get that spirit award!" said Jade.

"I certainly am not! I just want to make sure they're all settling in. I wish that seniors had taken an interest in me my junior year."

"Well, after 'the incident,' can you really blame them?"

"What was 'the incident'?" asked Penny.

"We're not talking about that," said Logan. "Especially not with *her.*"

"Our first year, Logan was really homesick," said Missy.

"I'm sorry, didn't I just ask that we *not* tell this story!"

"Everyone who wants to tell the Logan Worthe 'incident' story say 'aye.'"

"Aye," said the girls.

"It's unanimous!"

"Since when did this become a democracy?"

"It's a campocracy!"

"Whatever. Anyway, get your stories straight if you're going to tell it: I wasn't homesick. I'm never homesick. Because I never see my parents anyway."

"Wah-wah."

"Way to be sensitive."

"What?"

"Lo-Wo, do you really not want us to tell this story?"

"I just had a horrible bunk that year," said Logan. "It was before we were all together. I don't like to think about it."

"They didn't like her," said Jade.

"They didn't 'get' me."

"Whatever, Lo-Wo."

"So, anyway—"

"Do we really have to tell this story?"

"I think it will make Penny feel better about being homesick."

"Who said I was homesick?" asked Penny.

"Who said we need to make her feel better?" asked Logan.

"Do you want to hear the story or not?" asked Jade.

"Yeah, okay," Penny said, trying so hard to be cool and nonchalant.

"So, Logan was miserable—"

"My bunk mates ate all my food that I had artfully hidden," explained Logan.

"Logan missed the day in kindergarten when they taught everyone to share."

"I've gotten much better!"

"So, Logan decided to overdose . . . on Flintstones vitamins."

"I was *trying* to prove a point!"

"You were *trying* to get attention!"

Penny, on the other hand, was *trying* to cover up a smile.

"But you didn't do it, right?" Penny asked.

"Oh, she did it, all right," said Willow.

"So, what happened? Did you need to have your stomach pumped?"

"Tell her what happened, Logan," said Missy.

"I got the runs."

"What? We can't hear you."

"I got the runs!"

"She didn't just get the runs," said Gabby.

"She got the rainbow runs!" said Tess.

Penny couldn't believe it: Logan Worthe, Perfect-Popular-Queen-Bee-of-Lakefield-Academy Logan Worthe, had the rainbow runs? The Logan Worthe who Penny knew—or at the very least, knew *of*—would never tolerate this kind of treatment. It was all just too ridiculous: the Flintstones vitamins, the runs, the most popular girl in school being treated like a normal person. . . . The girls were laughing, and Penny couldn't help but laugh right along with them.

"We're not laughing at you, we're laughing with you," said Willow.

"Yeah, but . . . I'm not laughing," said Logan.

"It's funny!" said Gabby. "It was eight years ago! Can't you laugh at it now?"

"You're not the one who had to substitute Kaopectate for candy canteen for a week! It was devastating."

"Canteeeeeeeeeeeen!" yelled the girls.

"What's canteen?" asked Penny.

"You get canteen usually three or four times a week. It's basically like a little candy store and you get your choice of junk food. I like getting a Charleston Chew because it's the most bang for your buck. But that's just me," said Gabby.

"So, Logan, you lost candy canteen because you tried to overdose?"

"Well, when you put it like that, it just sounds ridiculous."

"But that's what happened, right?"

"Basically, yes."

Just before they arrived at Bunk One, Logan pulled Penny aside.

"Any of this gets out at Lakefield, and you are over, do you hear me?"

"Loud and clear, Rainbow Brite," said Penny.

Penny couldn't believe what she had just said, and to whom she had said it!

"Be careful, Moore. You have no idea what you're dealing with," warned Logan.

CAMP RULE #9

Fern Lake ladies never pass gas
(and they certainly do not use
said gas—should they pass it—
as a weapon).

When the girls got back to Bunk One after cookie line, Penny's mattress-roll-up was finally dry, so she decided to put sheets on it and accept the fact that this was really her bed (until Visiting Day at least), so she might as well make it as cozy as possible.

After helping Willow with her planting for a while, she decided to go down to tennis with Tess, where Penny ended up having a one-on-one session with Dirk the Jerk. She had played tennis a couple of times before, but she wasn't very good at it. She watched Tess, dripping with sweat as she did grueling running drills, and rallying with the head of the tennis department. But Penny couldn't help feeling that there was something missing from Tess's game. While she was clearly driven and determined, it seemed like her heart just wasn't in it. Penny looked away from Tess just in time for Dirk the Jerk to hit her leg with a ball.

"Head's up, sweetheart. You're slower than a dissolving tablet!" he yelled.

"Yeah, well, you're a pill," said Penny under her breath.

"What was that?"

"Nothing."

Before lunch, girls streamed into the living room to get their snail mail. All the Bunk One girls seemed to have quickly gotten over their e-mail and instant-message withdrawal, and Tess said she was relieved and excited about the novelty of reading "old-fashioned" mail. Penny could see campers running into the main house as she was walking up the hill with Tess—whose uniform was soaked through with sweat. Tess's cheeks were flushed, but her hair was still tied back perfectly. She had her racket bag over her shoulder. Penny noticed how strong her arms were and that her posture was perfect. This immediately made Penny stand up straighter, just like her mother always reminded her to do.

"You were really great . . . at the tennis," stammered Penny. "I mean, you're a great tennis player."

"Thanks. I certainly play enough."

"Do you like it?"

"Like what?"

"Tennis? I mean, you seem so dedicated to it."

"Um. Do I like it? I never really thought about it that way. My parents like it. It's important to them."

"But is it important to you?"

"Yeah, I guess, because it's important to them, so it's important to me, and vice versa. It's that whole 'what came first?' scenario."

"The chicken or the egg?"

"Exactly."

"So, which is it?"

"I'm too chicken to stand up to my parents."

"Gotcha," said Penny. "So, what's your favorite activity aside from tennis?"

"I don't get there much, but I really like the art shops. I took a life drawing class in school this year and I loved it . . . but then I had to drop it because of my training schedule. So," Tess said, changing the topic, "how was hitting with Dirk the Jerk?"

"He called me sweetheart."

"He called Annie sweetheart, too. Maybe calling females 'sweetheart' is his 'thing'?"

"He said I was slower than a dissolving tablet."

"Well, that can't be good."

"No. Probably not."

"You guys! I got a letter from my boyfriend!" yelled

Missy. She was leaning over the railing of the porch and waving the letter over her head like a flag.

"Is it slutty?" yelled Tess.

"I don't know! I haven't opened it yet! But I would bet it is!"

"We'll be right there," said Tess. "Come on, Penny! You gotta beat that dissolving tablet!"

Tess took Penny's hand and started to run toward the porch. Penny took a breath, and sprinted to keep up.

Lunch was another semi-inedible meal, so Penny made herself a peanut butter and jelly sandwich, which she washed down with blue "bug juice." Peanut butter and jelly seemed to be the "go-to" food at camp, which was just fine with Penny. Missy did a dramatic reading of the letter from her boyfriend. It was pretty short and not "slutty" (whatever "slutty" meant at this point anyway), but Missy liked to add a healthy dose of innuendo to each and every word, which, at the very least, kept it interesting.

After lunch was rest hour, during which Penny watched Missy shave her legs out of a fuchsia bucket on the back step of the bunk. Missy wore only a pink Jogbra and boy-shorts underwear that said WHERE'S SUNDAY? across the butt.

"So what is your preferred method of hair removal, Penny?" asked Missy. "There are so many options now—of course not all of them can be maintained at camp. Electrolysis, for example. You simply can't maintain the electrolysis at camp. I would bet that they don't even have the necessary voltage in Maine."

"Well, my mom taught me to shave last year, but it freaks me out . . . so I don't do it very often."

"Really? Why? I mean, doesn't your boyfriend like your legs to be smooth?"

"Um, I don't have a boyfriend."

"Oh. Boyfriends are great. But, like hair removal, they require a lot of upkeep."

"I'll remember that."

"Well, maybe we'll wax your legs later this week. And we could do a little something with your eyebrows."

"But, it's an all-girls camp. I mean, who cares?"

"Exactly. What better time to experiment with new looks?"

Penny hated to admit it, but maybe Missy had a point. And, Penny figured, it wouldn't hurt to have a new look to go along with her new camp persona.

"What are you slut-masters doing out here?"

Gabby had come out the back door with a small tub of Crystal Light fruit punch powder mix, which she ate "à la carte," dipping her index finger into the little plastic container and then sucking the powder off her finger. No pesky glass of water needed. Gabby's finger was already a bright shade of red. Missy leaned over while Gabby was in middip, and then sucked the powder off of Gabby's finger.

"Yum," said Missy.

"Dude!" yelled Gabby. "You totally just got shaving cream in my Crystal Light! Gross!"

Before Missy could respond, Willow emerged from the side of the bunk. She had a big, floppy straw hat, and a hoe. There was dirt all over her uniform.

"It's Will-hoe!" said Jade, emerging from the bunk.

"That right there just cost you zucchini privileges for the rest of the summer!" said Willow.

Logan came out with Annie right behind her.

"Now that's hardly egalitarian, Willow," said Logan.

"I'm a humanist," said Willow.

"Huh?" asked Gabby.

"Be careful, Willow," said Annie. "Even humanists aren't allowed to bunk hop."

"During rest hour and after lights out, campers are bunk bound," explained Missy.

"But I'm just planting a garden right next to the bunk!"

"Sorry, Will, but you know the rules: take one step off this back porch and you're officially bunk hopping!"

"If we're caught outside of our bunks by one of the counselors on rest hour/night duty, we lose canteen."

"Losing canteen seems to be the punishment for everything," said Penny.

"That or you're sent home."

"Yeah, but you have to, like, murder someone to be sent home."

Penny and Logan shared a look.

"We'll see about that," said Logan.

Later that night, Penny's butt was hurting from sitting on so many benches, and she knew there were more to come that evening. After dinner, they went back to their bunks, put sweatshirts on, and got ready for another night in UTC. Bunk One decided to wear the exact same thing (their aforementioned Bunk One matching sweats, which Penny did not have) and braided pigtails. The girls linked arms and walked out of the bunk toward UTC. Willow was the last one out and looked over her shoulder at Penny.

"You coming, Penny?" she asked.

"Let's just go, Willow," said Logan.

"I'm right behind you guys."

Penny savored the few moments she had to herself. While the girls were possibly not as bad as she had initially thought, being with them almost twenty-four-seven was exhausting. Maybe it was just Logan and the idea of breaking rules and getting kicked out that was exhausting? Penny looked around the bunk. Now there were towels hanging over the rafters and camp uniform shirts hanging over the doors of cubbies. It already looked fully lived-in. It was weird to think that they had just arrived the day before. It felt like a lifetime to Penny. She walked out to see the rest of Bunk One up ahead with younger girls trailing behind them at a respectful distance.

At UTC, Barb and George read letters written by the previous summer's Bunk One girls. The letters described how when they got to FLC as eight-year-olds, they had no idea how it would change the course of the rest of their lives. They said they would carry Fern Lake Camp and the people they met there in their hearts forever. They said that they would miss the wind through the trees, the steam rising off the lake in the morning, Jon insisting on one cookie at cookie line, the amazing girls they had met who still inspired them and were in their thoughts and hearts even during the grueling "standardized test that shall not be named." They would miss going to sleep every night and waking up every morning in a bunk with their best friends. They repeated over and over how lucky every camper was to be receiving the great gift of camp, and how they were jealous, because they still missed it every day. The Bunk One letters were punctuated by laughs and sighs and cheers and yes, even tears.

The letters pointed out what Penny had been witnessing firsthand: these girls around her weren't robots or Stepford campers, these girls were all quite unique, but what they shared was this bizarre and undying love for camp. The girls looked at one another around UTC with big smiles.

"Psssst."

Penny looked around.

"Psssst."

Where was that coming from?

"Hey, Penmeister, down here."

Penny looked between and below the bleachers only to find Paxton underneath with a packet of Twizzlers.

"Twizzler?"

"Paxton! What are you doing under there?" asked Penny.

"I just like the view."

"Paxton, go back to your seat."

"Hey, Penny . . ."

"Yeah?"

Without saying a word, Paxton winked dramatically at her.

"You've gotta be kidding me," said Penny.

But Paxton didn't seem to be going anywhere no matter how much she shooed him away. So, Penny had a crazy idea. It wasn't something that would get her sent home, really, but it certainly might be in that rule-breaker/troublemaker category she was fitting into so easily here—and which was actually becoming kind of fun. She would never do this in her real high school life. But this wasn't her high school, even if the Queen Bee was sitting in the very same row. This was camp. And at camp, even the Queen Bee wasn't so perfect. Penny wouldn't be there for much longer anyway (if Logan had anything to do with it), so who cared? Penny would deal with Logan's Lakefield wrath in September. But until then, she was going to have fun and break some rules, gosh darn it! Penny reached across Willow and Tess to tap Gabby's arm.

"You eat the beans tonight?" Penny whispered.

"Of course. Why?"

"Under the bench," Penny said through a locked jaw. Gabby looked down covertly. Paxton saluted Gabby and winked again.

"Do it for your bunk," said Penny. "Do it for your camp!"

Gabby got real serious-looking and nodded.

"I'll do it! Switch with me."

Penny slid over, and Gabby carefully moved across Willow and Tess, who were curious as to what was going on.

"Is this a game of musical bleachers or something?" asked Tess.

"Shhh," said Gabby.

Gabby sat down right above where Paxton was hiding. Penny gave her the thumbs-up. And with a very determined facial expression, Gabby clenched her fists, closed her eyes, and scrunched her face, until . . .

"Oh, Jesus Christ! My eyes! My nose!" yelled Paxton.

Paxton blindly ran out from underneath the bleachers. He was covering his face and wretching dramatically.

"Silent, but deadly!" said Gabby, as she high-fived Penny.

"Paxton! What are you doing under the bleachers?" asked Barb.

"Still enjoying the view, Paxton?" Penny asked.

"You girls are asking for it!" he said. "You haven't seen the last of me!"

CAMP RULE #10

Fern Lake ladies never paddle alone.

The next night at dinner, Bunk One was still laughing about the Paxton farting incident. Penny was a hero. Gabby was a hero. Fun was had by all. All, except for Logan . . . and Paxton, of course. Penny was, slowly but surely, becoming accepted by the group, and Logan could do nothing to stop it. In fact, it seemed that in her rule breaking, Penny was beginning to discover a new side of herself.

"Where do you think Paxton learns that kind of bad behavior?" asked Tess.

"Yeah, George is so, like, docile."

Penny was listening intently until she saw a male figure through the front screen door. He was wearing a white T-shirt and khaki cutoffs. His T-shirt was just tight enough so that she could tell there was a strong muscular body underneath it. He was wearing old-school Ray-Ban sunglasses and didn't take them off, even though he was already inside, and had surveyed the dining hall.

"Who's that?" Penny barely managed to squeeze the words out.

"My future husband," said Missy.

"I guess your relationship really is monotonous?" said Gabby.

"Don't be slutty!" said Missy.

"Is that . . ."

"Couldn't be . . ."

"Hey, Cameron!" said Annie.

"Annie! No! I haven't showered since I got here!"

"Are you mad, woman? My hair isn't straightened!" said Gabby.

Cameron looked over, and raised his eyebrows at Annie. He sauntered over to Table One. Annie stood up to give Cameron a hug. How Penny wished she could be Annie at that moment.

"Hey, Annie. Haven't seen you since . . ."

His voice was the sexiest thing Penny had ever heard. It was like a deep nasally grinding sound that just happened to be coated in ambrosia.

"Four summers ago, when we were just wild fifteen-year-olds," said Annie. "You know, you can't keep me away from this place. Are you back for the summer?"

"Nah, just for a few days. We'll see how it goes. Look,

Barbara's about to lose it because I'm not supposed to be 'fraternizing' with the campers after . . . *what happened*. So I'll catch you later?"

"Sure."

"Girls," he said. He nodded his head to the table and sauntered away as casually as he had sauntered in.

"I love you," Gabby mouthed as he left.

"I haven't seen him in years!" said Logan.

"Okay, can you girls keep a secret?" asked Annie.

"Um, do Fern Lake ladies love Fern Lake Camp?"

"Yeah!" they yelled.

The girls leaned in.

"Well, spill it!" said Logan. "What's the deal-yo?"

"That's Cameron."

"Who? What? Can someone please fill me in here?" asked Penny.

"Cameron is Paxton's older brother."

"He's a real 'bad boy.' Been thrown out of every board-ing school in the country. He probably got thrown out of another summer program or job or something, and that's why he's here. The last time he got thrown out of a summer program, four years ago, he came here and . . . well, let's just say, it didn't end well."

"Why?"

"Cameron got 'involved' with a girl in my bunk," said Annie.

"Did she say he was a good kisser?" asked Missy. "Did you see those lips!?"

"So? What happened?"

"Well, he disappeared, and I guess he hasn't been allowed back at camp since."

"And your bunk mate?"

"She got kicked out of camp."

Gasps were heard from every corner of Table One.

"Kicked out of camp?"

"Oh, the humanity!" said Willow.

"Awful, just awful," said Gabby.

"Who was it?"

"Well, it was four years ago, so you guys were like total babies. Her name was Amy."

"I remember her! She was my camp big sister! But everyone said she went home because she had a family emergency!"

"That's what they always say when they have to send a girl home," said Annie.

"Wow. He *is* cute."

"Yeah, but no boy is cute enough to get thrown out of camp for, that's for sure," said Willow.

Logan kicked Penny under the table at the mention of being thrown out of camp, but Penny barely felt it. Penny's mind was racing. No boys looked like Cameron in her school. No boys looked like Cameron in Penny's dreams, for

crying out loud! *Hoorah hoorah hoorah, Cameron!* Now, that
was something to cheer for. Penny watched him intently as
he walked over to the head table. Paxton ran up to him and
hugged his legs.

Penny had her toothbrush and was on her way to scrub
underneath the docks at the waterfront the next day. She
didn't really believe the punishment fit the crime, but it
was not her decision. Penny couldn't stop thinking about
Cameron. Who would have thought she would have to come
to an all-girls camp to have a major crush on a boy?

On her way across the little beach that led to the waterfront, Penny heard something coming from the water ski
shed. She decided to look inside. Pairs of water skis and
wake boards were lined up against both walls, and life jack-
ets were on a rack next to ski ropes and other ski accessories.
She pulled one slalom ski off the wall and examined it.

"Aren't you supposed to be in your bunk?"

Penny looked over to see Cameron standing in the doorway of the shed. At which point, she promptly dropped the
ski directly on her own foot.

"Ow!"

"Now, that had to hurt. You okay?"

Cameron leaned over to help her. The weight of the ski
crushing her foot at any other time would probably have
caused her a great deal of pain. Possibly some tears. Defi-

nitely some complaining. But at that moment, Penny Moore couldn't feel a thing. She blinked and hoped that she wasn't just imagining that Cameron was shirtless. He stood up and placed the ski back on the rack. And then he took off his sunglasses, and stared right at her. His eyes were bright green, like the algae she was about to scrub off the dock with her toothbrush.

"Hello?" he asked again.

It was as if his words came straight from the depths of his soul up through his nasal passages and out into the world where they actually coated Penny and everything around them with a warm blanket of wonderfulness and perfection.

"Hi," she said.

"So, what brings you down here?"

"Oh, you know . . ."

"Where are my manners? Do you want a soda?"

"You have soda?"

"Sure. Oh, unless you're worried about getting caught with it. I forget that stuff is contraband for you girls."

"Yeah, so do I. I don't even really drink soda at home, but now that it's so forbidden, I'm dying for one."

"Funny how that works."

"Yeah."

Cameron reached into an orange cooler and threw her a Coke. It was ice cold. She tapped the top of the can three times—a habit she had acquired after her cousin told her it would prevent soda from spraying all over. That must have been a myth because as she opened it, it exploded every-where. *Smooth*.

"Here, take this." Cameron threw Penny a shirt that had been hanging on the door.

"I don't want to . . ."

"It's okay, really. I need to wash it anyway."

"Thanks."

Penny used Cameron's T-shirt to wipe the soda off her face and arms. The fact that his navy blue name tag had been sewn inside the collar, well, that just made him all the more . . . human. And Penny *loved* humans.

"Well, thanks. I should get back," she said.

"Don't want to get caught 'bunk hopping,'" he said. "I hear missing canteen is a drag."

"Yeah, that's the word on the street. I mean, on the road. Or the lake, or, the street."

"Why are you down here anyway? And why do you have your toothbrush?"

"I have to go clean the docks. I snuck under them when I was supposed to be swimming rectangles."

"Check you out. I had my first kiss under those docks."

"Really? I mean, cool. I should go, so . . . I'll catch you later."

Penny turned around to leave, and then she had a thought . . .

"Hey, Cameron?"

"Yeah?"

"Just out of curiosity, what kind of thing might a girl have to do to get kicked out of a camp like this?"

"Breathe without cheering?"

"Seriously," she said. "I mean, just out of curiosity, of course."

"Of course. Well, you've come to the right man. I've been kicked out of more boarding schools than I can count."

"Maybe that's why you got kicked out?"

"I like you." He laughed. "What's a girl like you doing in a camp like this?"

"Parents blindsided me."

"Rough. Well, camp is all about rules, so just pick one and break it."

"Sounds easy enough."

"Why? You in the market for some rules to break?"

"Maybe," Penny said. *Who was she?*

"Well, don't tell anyone where you got that."

"Got what?"

"The soda?"

"Oh, right."

"Come back sometime. I'll teach you to ski. If I stick around."

"I will," she said. "If I stick around."

And then in her coolest exit yet, Penny held up her can of Coke to Cameron, as if it were a toast, and promptly tripped over her own foot, landing face-first in the sand.

Penny was back at the waterfront the next afternoon for the required canoeing and kayaking "tips and dumps." The girls had to wear big, orange life preservers around their necks. They were also required to wear old running shoes into the water so that they wouldn't cut their feet on the canoes, or on jagged shells on the bottom of the lake. Penny's sneakers quickly filled up with water and sand and lake muck, which was particularly uncomfortable.

Mike Canoe would be taking them through the drills. For kayaking, they had to capsize one by one while staying in the little well of the kayak until Mike brought them back up to the surface. There was so much water up Penny's nose by the time she came up that she was convinced her eyeballs looked like shaken snow in a snow globe.

For canoeing, three girls had to capsize the whole canoe together by rocking it back and forth several times and finally turning it over. At first, Penny liked kayaking more than canoeing simply because it seemed more manageable: she liked the idea of being able to work (or paddle, in this case) alone, and not having to depend on anyone else.

Mike Canoe stood in the water with his heavily ringed hands on his hips. He was the last person anyone would ever imagine being a counselor at an expensive all-girls camp. He was enormous (in attitude and stature). He had several tattoos and wore skull-and-crossbones rings and necklaces. At first glance, Penny thought Mike would certainly be better suited to perching on a Harley, instead of in a canoe. But according to Jade, Mike had been there way before any of them had arrived at FLC. He complained about the girls being princesses and he took no bull from anyone, but he loved FLC unconditionally and returned every summer.

"Come on, girls. What are you, juniors?" he barked.

"How dare you!" said Missy.

"We're trying!" said Tess.

"Gabby, you're not rocking the boat enough!"

"Oh yeah, that's nice, Mike," said Gabby. "Pick on the fat girl?"

"Is that *phat* with a *ph*?" asked Jade.

But before Gabby could finish her rant, Mike tipped their canoes over himself. Gabby, Missy, and Tess screamed as they tumbled into the water. Logan, Willow, and Jade were laughing from their canoe until the girls swam over and tipped them over, too. And Penny watched the commotion from her kayak. She was dry, but she was alone. Penny watched the girls swimming and laughing and splashing together. It was the first time she started to feel like maybe it wouldn't be so bad to be a part of this camp-thing after all.

And suddenly, her wish came true (kind of). Penny was soaking wet. Gabby and Tess had tipped over her kayak when she wasn't looking. Penny was realizing that, at camp, working alone (and staying dry) was really overrated.

CAMP RULE #11

*Fern Lake ladies always
play their best . . . or they
do not play at all.*

As the next few days at camp came and went, Penny
was starting to get used to (maybe even to enjoy!) the comfort of the camp routine. She even had to admit that her
mattress-roll-up had become surprisingly comfortable.
Although, of course, she didn't know how long it would
last, since Logan was trying to find an acceptable way of getting Penny sent home.

By the day of their first competition of the summer—a
swim meet—all the girls were ready for it, with spirit to
burn. Logan was unusually quiet that morning. She ate a
light breakfast and didn't talk at all. Willow guessed that
Logan still got nervous before swim meets because she put
so much pressure on herself to win.

It was a beautiful day with barely a cloud in the sky and
the sun shining brightly overhead. The camp had been split

into two teams for the meet: the tan team and the green team. Bunk One would be split to lead each team. Willow, Missy, Jade, and Penny would lead the Tan Team, while Gabby, Tess, and Logan would lead the Green Team.

Willow had painted a feather a tan color and had it sticking up from her headband.

"You do realize you're wearing a disease, right?" asked Jade.

"What doesn't kill me makes me stronger," said Willow.

"Biiiiiiiird fluuuuuu," said Jade in a high singsong voice.

"You are so immature, Jade!"

The teams cheered from their own sides of the beach. But before the races began, apparently, it was a tradition that the girls dressed the male waterfront counselors in team clothes . . . *female* team clothes.

There was Gary Sailing, who wore white zinc on his nose and lips; he always got it all over everything, including his twin brother, Bruce Sailing. There was the waterfront "rover," Glenn, who often carried his guitar with him as he . . . well, as he roved. And then there was Cameron. How a guy could get dressed up in drag and still remain the epitome of masculinity was beyond Penny. His features were angular, and his eyes were always half-closed in a very sexy, perpetually-too-relaxed-to-really-care-and-just-throw-me-out-of-schools-and-summer-programs-if-you-don't-like-it kind of way.

Mike Canoe was tough to dress because he was so big and burly. So, Willow cut up a burlap sack and belted it. He looked more like an angry medieval monk than a woman, but it gave all the girls immense enjoyment nonetheless. They dressed male counselors up in skirts and dresses and beads and visors and hats with large brims. The Green Team even dressed the Sailing Twins in matching green wigs and tutus.

But the sweet, sensitive, and soft-spoken water rover, Glenn, really got the brunt of the drag. The girls dressed him in a tan-colored pencil skirt and a tan off-the-shoulder peasant blouse. Penny truly believed that no man (or woman, for that matter) should ever have to wear a pencil skirt. Penny saved a tasteful tank top for Cameron (if she just had to look at his perfect muscular arms all day, well, so be it, she'd suffer for her team), and a loose hula skirt that he could wear over his khakis. Missy flirtingly put a tiara on him, but Penny took it off when she wasn't looking and put it on Water Rover Glenn instead. After all, Penny thought, no self-respecting man can wear a tan pencil skirt without a matching tiara. *Naturally*.

The male waterfront staff along with the all-female swim staff organized the races and kept the times of all the swimmers. The campers swam by age group, and the Bunk One girls and Penny cheered from the end of each lane.

When not cheering from the docks, the girls took part in the sand sculpture competition on the beach.

The Tan Team made a huge sand sculpture of a dove (the bird and its design were Willow's ideas, "because it's so much more than a sand sculpture, it's a statement about peace"). Tess—who was happily covered in sand and immersed in the construction—had designed an elaborate dinosaur for the Green Team. Her tennis racket was abandoned by the lawn to the side of the beach, and she didn't seem to miss it one bit.

Penny stopped for a moment to take in the scene before her: male counselors were running around in pencil skirts and tiaras with stopwatches, men in tutus and dripping with colored costume jewelry and zinc oxide were trying to be taken semiseriously as they shot the start gun and fiddled with their earplugs. Mike was in a burlap sack, and a very feminine "tan" colored wig, accessorized with his own rings and tattoos.

"*Crush* her!" he yelled.

Slowly but surely, Penny was learning the cheers. Most importantly—as she stood among Bunk One at the finish line of the swim lanes, cheering for her team—she found herself screaming just as loudly as all the other girls. Girls were swimming and cheering their hearts out in a way Penny had never seen (and certainly never done) before.

And then it was Penny's turn to swim: it was just Logan and Penny, racing the crawl stroke. The two girls got into diving positions in front of their lanes, and Penny looked over at Logan.

"Good luck," said Penny.

Logan responded with an exaggerated eye roll. Penny, hurt but not surprised, shrugged it off and looked straight ahead. Penny may not have had the best form, but she knew she was a fast swimmer. The gun went off, and the girls dove in. Penny could see Logan pulling ahead out of the corner of her eye. It was Penny's instinct to speed up and try to overtake her, but whether it was because she knew how important winning was to Logan or because she just wanted Logan to like her (or maybe a bit of both), she remained a stroke behind. It was not anything terribly noticeable, but it was just enough to let Logan take the lead. Logan won the race by two strokes.

Both Logan and Penny were breathing hard when they reached the finish line. Penny smiled her biggest Fern Lake lady smile and reached her hand out to Logan.

"Nice race," said Penny.

"Don't 'nice race' me," said Logan.

"What?"

"I don't want your pity, Penny! Okay? When you swim or play anything here, you do your best. I would rather lose fairly than win because you felt sorry for me."

"But I didn't—"

Logan took off her white cap, and held it up. "Do you see this? This took me seven summers to get. Seven summers! Do you know how many times I came to free swim, how many laps I had to do until I could swim without making a damn ripple in the water? How much fun bonding time with my friends I missed because I was down here obsessed with this? You couldn't know, because you weren't here. Play your best, Moore, or don't play at all."

From the dock, Jade extended her hand to Logan, who reached up and took it. Gabby went behind Jade, grabbed her waist, and together they pulled Logan out of the water. Penny felt like she had just been kicked in the stomach. Here she was, just trying to do the right thing, the spirited thing, by letting Logan win. The whole day of feeling like she was a part of something was an illusion. She wasn't a part of anything. She was more alone than ever.

But then she felt something on her head: it was Willow's hand.

"Come on, Pen," said Willow.

Willow extended her hand to Penny from the dock. Missy came up behind Willow to help her pull Penny up and out of the water. But Missy was easily distracted, especially by the likes of the Sailing Twins, who at that moment just happened to be changing out of their drag costumes behind the sailing shed.

BARRINGTON PUBLIC LIBRARY
BARRINGTON, R.I.

"Oh, my!" said Missy. "That's not monotonous at all!"

Missy put her hand over her mouth, accidentally letting go of Willow just as she was leaning down to help Penny, which caused Penny to pull Willow into the lake by accident. Willow surfaced with her wet feather plastered on her forehead.

"Missy! That was really very irresponsible, unthoughtful, and . . . well, slutty!" said Willow.

"Oh! Was that my fault? Sorry, Will," said Missy.

"Man overboard!" yelled Sherry. She whistled loudly and threw a life preserver into the water. It hit Willow right on the head.

"Ow!" said Willow. "I'm not drowning, Sherry!"

"Then why aren't you wearing your cap?"

"Where did she learn her reasoning skills?" asked Willow.

"Well, *my* reasoning skills suggest that we just use the ladder," said Penny.

"Good idea," said Willow.

"I'm going to need that life preserver back," said Sherry.

Willow and Penny put their mouths underwater to disguise their giggles as they swam toward the ladder.

"Come on, we have to do our final cheers."

"There are more?" Penny asked.

"Oh, there are always more cheers," said Willow.

When they got back to the beach, the Tan Team faced the Green Team. The Green Team began:

"When Bunk One yells, they yell with all their might:
Green Team, go out and fight, get there and do it right!
We'll do the best for the Green team,
For the Green Team
Sis boom bah Green Team rah!"

"You ready?" asked Jade.

"Ready as I'll ever be," said Penny.

"Just remember what we taught you," said Willow.

They began screaming with what voices they had left.

"We, the Tan Team, would like to show you,
Our spirit, hit it:
Say hey hey hey,
Say hey hey hey.
Whatchya got to say?
Whatchya got to say?
We're big and bad and victory bound,
We'll stomp your team right to the ground!
Say hey hey hey,
The Tan Team's on their way, hey!"

In fact, Penny screamed so loud and for so long, that at the end of the day, she barely had any voice left at all. The girls sounded like frogs croaking, or Demi Moore . . . talking. They gathered their towels, sunscreen, and tan and green belongings, and started walking up the hill until Penny realized that she had forgotten the team clipboard at the waterfront. She ran back down to get it, but the dock was roped off and no one was there . . . at least, it seemed like no one was there at first.

"Looking for this?"

Penny turned around to see Paxton dressed in Green and Tan (apparently, he didn't like taking sides), carrying the team clipboard.

"Yes, actually I was. Thanks, Paxton."

"Nice lineup," he said.

"Thanks."

"We have to stop meeting like this."

"Like what?" asked Penny.

"You know, like . . . this."

She grabbed the clipboard from him.

"Thanks, Paxton . . . I gotta go."

"Hey, Penny! I was wondering if you'd like to have dinner with me and my parents tonight?"

"Thanks, Paxton. But . . . I'm assigned to sit with my bunk."

"Maybe another time then, Penny?"

"Sure. I'll just take a rain check."

"Don't think I won't cash in on that soon. I keep track of that sort of thing. I have an abacus. You should come see it sometime."

"I'll get right on that."

Penny turned around and started the walk back up the hill again.

"Hey, Penny."

"Paxton! I really have to get back to . . ."

But it wasn't Paxton at all this time. It was Cameron. Big brother was emerging from the counselor lounge, and he was no longer dressed in drag.

"Oh, hi," said Penny.

"Sorry about my brother. I think he has a thing for you."

"I'm a little old for him, don't you think?" asked Penny.

"But what is age anyway?"

"Yeah."

"Anyway, I just wanted to thank you for taking it easy on me today. Not sure the tiara would have been my style."

"Yeah. Tiaras are so last year."

"My thoughts exactly. You walking up the hill?"

"Um, yeah. You?"

"Yup." They both stood in place awkwardly. "So, should we . . ."

"Walk! Yes. Let's walk!"

They walked up to the head of campus, just a few feet from Bunk One.

"So, this is me. Where do you live?"

"With my folks for now. I'm not sure how much longer I'll be here."

"Ah."

"So, I guess I'll see you around, Penny."

"Yeah. It's a pretty good bet."

A shutter slammed, and Penny heard the distinct sound of girls giggling. *Oh no.* Bunk One had seen Cameron and Penny together. Penny ran in to try to do damage control. But it was too late. They were already shrieking by the time Penny entered the bunk.

"Guys, please don't make a big deal out of this! We were just talking."

"A likely story!"

"Girls, would you mind if I had a moment alone with Penny?" asked Logan.

"Look out, Penny's hot stuff . . . she's a rule breaker!"

"She's my slutty hero!" said Missy.

"I'm not slutty!" Penny protested. "Okay, maybe just a little."

Jade solemnly stepped forward and put her hand on her heart.

"I'm slutty," she said.

"I'm slutty," said Tess.

"I'm slutty," said Gabby.

One by one, the girls came forward. Except Logan.

"Come on, Logan," said Missy. "Don't be a spoilsport. You can be the sluttiest of us all."

"At least that's what it says on the bathroom walls at Lakefield!" blurted Penny.

In theory, it was a funny line. It was meant to be a joke. But instead, silence befell Bunk One.

"I was just . . . I was joking . . . ," began Penny.

But Penny didn't finish her explanation because Logan grabbed Penny's wrist and dragged her out the back of the bunk.

"What the hell was that?"

"I was kidding!"

"That is *exactly* what I have been talking about since the first day. This is not Lakefield. This is camp! This is supposed to be a haven from that! It was the only place left where people treated me like a normal person, where I could be myself, not the Logan who has to look great for school every day, or throw the best parties, or go out with the hottest guys who tell lies about how far I've gone with them. No one writes mean things on bathroom walls here. There are no labels here that stick with you the way there are in high school. You think that Jade and I or Willow and I would ever be friends in high school? Not a chance. But here it doesn't matter that Gabby has irritable bowel syndrome and Willow's a hippie or a hippelectual or whatever it is she calls herself this summer. This is exactly why I didn't want you coming in here and reminding us, reminding *me*, of reality. This was supposed to be my last summer to enjoy that, and now I can't," said Logan.

"I'm sorry I said that, Logan. But you have to know that I was kidding."

"I don't *have* to do anything. Don't tell me that now you want to stay or something? We had a deal."

"Sure, I still want to leave," said Penny.

"Well, then, it seems you've found all on your own a perfect way to get kicked out."

"Cameron?"

"Uh, yeah?"

"But I don't want to get anyone else in trouble . . . and I would really rather not look like a total ho-bag in front of the whole camp."

"And all this time, I was trying to come up with some creative way of getting you sent home, and you were doing something illegal all along. Penny Moore, you are full of surprises!"

"I wasn't doing anything illegal! Nothing is going on with Cameron and me!"

"We'll see about that."

Logan brushed past Penny, purposely bumping her shoulder as she walked back into the bunk.

CAMP RULE #12

Fern Lake ladies never panic.

It was significantly quieter than usual in the dining room the night of the swim meet—every girl was sunburned, exhausted, and literally speechless from all the yelling and cheering they had done. Bunk One slurped hot water with wedges of lemon so that they would have their voices back for the next day. Gabby ended up dumping almost an entire jar of honey into her water—and her lap—and then got it on Missy, who started licking her own hands.

"It's amazing to me that you never fail to turn everything into something sexual," said Jade.

"What do you mean?" Missy asked with her tongue glued to her palm.

"Sound the Missy alarm, anything with a puuuuu-uuulse!!!" screamed the girls.

Missy then whispered to Jade who whispered to Gabby

who whispered to Tess and so on. Suddenly, they started doing their shushing thing, where they put their index fingers to their lips and held up their hands. The room quickly became silent.

"Sound the Penny Moore alarm, Caaaaaaameron!"

Penny turned red and slumped down in her seat on the bench.

"You guys, he's just a friend!" Penny said, to no avail.

But just as she started to feel defensive and angry, she heard similar cheers coming from nearby tables:

"Let's all cheer, Laura Miller for spilling the bug juice everywhere. Rah rah, Laura!"

"Sound the Jill Weingarten alarm, Joe Archerrrrrrrrrr rrrrrry!"

"Her name is Amanda, check. She thinks she's cool, check. But we all know, check. She likes to drool, check!"

Penny watched as a girl whose "alarm" had been "sounded" turned her same shade of red. The girl laughed it off and then pushed the girl next to her off the bench. There was more laughter and smiles all around.

Stacy stood up in the middle of the dining room and shushed the camp.

"Hello, ladies! You will all be happy to know that I have the results from the swim meet," she said.

Campers gasped and sat forward on their benches in anticipation.

"Everyone swam like winners, but overall, the *actual* winner of this summer's swim meet is . . . the Tan Team!"

Jade, Willow, Missy, and Penny jumped up and hugged and screamed, "Hoorah Hoorah Hoorah, Tan!" Girls all over the dining room were yelling, hugging, and high-fiving until Stacy quieted everyone again. Logan maintained her patented Mc-Smile.

"Individual results will be posted on the front porch if anyone's interested."

After dinner, Penny watched as Logan broke through the little crowd that surrounded the posted swim meet results. She may have won, but she hadn't beaten her own record, and what's more, Penny knew that Logan couldn't help feeling that she didn't win it fair and square.

Penny took to heart what Logan had said about playing her best or not playing at all. Over the next few days, Penny did indeed play her heart out in every activity and sport, and was finding new strengths in different sports every day. In soccer, Penny played the defensive position of "sweeper." This meant that she just had to get the ball as far away from her own team's goal as possible, and kick it back onto the other side of the field. The sweeper position was given to the person with the strongest kick. Penny had a lot of power, she just had very little control of where the ball went. More often than not, the ball would fly far, but out of bounds. Logan, on the other hand, played center halfback, covering both offense and defense, and dribbled like David Beckham. The first few games, she easily dribbled around Penny and had clear shots at the goal. But as the days went on, Penny became more confident in her ability. She started to anticipate Logan's moves and was able to get the ball away from her before she had a shot at the goal. Penny was indeed playing her best, and she was giving Logan Worthe a run for her money.

After over a week of scheduled daily sports and activities, the girls were excited for a free night: they were actually allowed to do whatever they wanted. Many campers were rehearsing skits for the upcoming talent show. But Bunk One brought their radio outside and danced at the head of campus because . . . they were Bunk One, so every night was their talent show and anything they did was immediately considered cool. Penny sat on the steps of the bunk with her book, but she couldn't concentrate. She was no different from the rest of the girls in camp—she was watching the Bunk One girls and wishing she could be a part of their group, too. Missy got up on the bench and performed her slutty dance moves. The rest of the girls were just jumping around and being silly. The girls were especially rowdy because it was Annie's night off.

When they went back inside the bunk just moments before lights out, they noticed they had a visitor: it had wings, but it was definitely *not* a dove. Whatever this creature was, it probably ate doves for breakfast.

So, they did what any hot-blooded American girls would do: they panicked. And started screaming. Logan got the broom, Jade took the nearest tennis racket, and they both started swinging. Girls were laughing and crying at the same time.

"Not my new racket!" yelled Tess.

"It's going to suck our blood!" said Missy.

"Don't hurt it!" said Willow. "It's one of God's creatures!"

"It's a rat with wings, you hippie!" yelled Jade.

"I'm a hippelectual! And it has a right to live!" yelled Willow.

"*We* have a right to live!" yelled Gabby.

"Be free, Freebird! Be free! Fly like the wind, Freebird, fly!" screamed Willow.

"Let's all just calm down!" said Logan.

The scary winged creature dove kamikaze-style just past Logan's ear.

"AAAAAAAAAAAAAAAAH!" she screamed. "Out of the bunk! Out of the bunk! Out of the bunk nooooooo-oow!"

"It's going to kill us!" said Gabby. "We're all going to diiiiiiiiiiiiiiiiiiiiie!!!"

Penny may have screamed, too. Okay, yes, Penny definitely screamed. They ran outside as the other campers came out of their bunks to see what all the commotion was about. Stacy walked briskly toward them from her own house behind the softball field. Jade said that Stacy never ran because she believed that running implied panic, and Stacy didn't believe in panicking. Penny was amazed that even though Stacy's shirt was on backward and the fly on her uniform shorts was unzipped, she still managed to remember her faithful clipboard.

"Ladies . . . ladies . . . ladies! What is the problem here?"

They were all talking at once, so the only words that could be deciphered from the overlapping voices were:

"Rat."

"Wings."

"Rabies."

"Death."

"Blood."

"Vampires."

"End of the world as we know it."

"All right, ladies. Settle! Settlllllllle! I'm sure it's just a sweet little bird that got a little lost."

"That's what I said!" said Willow.

"I've never seen a bird like that," said Missy.

"He's probably much more afraid of us than we are of him."

"Speak for yourself," said Gabby.

Stacy confidently walked inside the bunk with her clipboard. Campers had flocked to the scene, and a hush fell over the crowd. As Stacy neared the bunk, all that could be heard was the jingle-jangle of the copious keys attached to her lanyard. She slowly walked up the Bunk One steps, opened the door, and stood in the doorway. She looked around the inside. Gabby took Penny's hand.

"I don't see anything here, ladies," said Stacy.

She shook her head, shrugged her shoulders, and flipped on the lights. At which point, the bat flew from the rafters, dive-bombed Stacy, missing her nose by barely a centimeter. She yelped, ducked, and quickly pivoted her body. Using her clipboard as a shield, she stayed low to the ground as she exited the bunk, slamming the door behind her.

"Okay, yeah. It's a bat. It's definitely . . . a bat. It's big. It's . . . big . . . a big . . . bat. BAT! It's okay. I got my clipboard. I'll take care of this. Just, wait here, girls. And do NOT open that door!"

Since the exterminator would not be able to come until the following day, the girls were "evacuated" from Bunk One that night and slept in tents on the softball field.

"It's like a slumber party!" said Gabby.

"Every night is a slumber party at camp," said Tess.

"They're not going to kill the freebird, are they?" asked Willow.

"I don't know," said Jade. "But I did hear something about it tasting delicious in a bug juice marinade."

"Ewwwww!"

"That's not funny!" said Willow.

Penny joined the girls as they coated themselves in bug spray and decided to forgo the tents to sleep out under the stars. Their sleeping bags had been rescued by the Sailing Twins, who had bravely run into the quarantined bunk wearing rain ponchos and using the lids of garbage cans as shields.

Just as the girls got into their sleeping bags, they heard a twig cracking. *Hadn't they filled their wildlife quotient*? But it was worse than wildlife: it was Paxton.

"Panty raid!" Paxton emerged from the darkness dressed in full camouflage pajamas with green and black crayon all over his face.

"Get out, Paxton!" said Jade.

"Panty raid!" he yelled again.

"Where does he learn this stuff?" asked Logan.

"Ever heard of cable television? Panty raid!"

Missy stood up and put her hand on her hip.

"Wait a second, girls. Doesn't a panty raid mean we get his panties, too?"

"Well, there *is* only one of him and seven of us."

"Wait, that's not how it's supposed to go," said Paxton.

Penny followed the others as they stood up on their sleeping bags.

"Panty raid!" yelled Logan.

"Uh, yeah. Um, it's getting a little late, girls. Way past my bedtime. But let's do this again soon?"

"How about in fifteen years?" yelled Logan.

Paxton sped away from the girls, running back to Barb and George's house, where he dove into the open first-floor window from which he had clearly escaped. The girls saw a light go on in the next room, and then the front door opened. Penny was sure it would be Barb or George, but then she recognized the swagger of the figure coming toward them, lit only by the moon.

"Is that who I think it is?" asked Gabby.

"Uh, yeah," said Missy. "It's Penny's husband."

"Shut up!" said Penny.

Gabby threw her pillow at Missy.

"Ow!" said Missy.

"It was a *pillow*," said Gabby.

"Be cool, girls," said Jade.

"This isn't what camp is about," said Logan. "He shouldn't be here. This makes me so angry. He's like the snake in the Garden of Eden."

They could hear his bare footsteps through the dewy grass.

"Hey, girls," said Cameron.

Each girl chirped some form of "hi" or "hey" or "what's up?" They were trying to be nonchalant. What Penny realized at that moment was that "nonchalant" does not exist at an all-girls camp when boys are involved. There was some giggling. There was definite blushing, not that anyone could see it in the dark. Logan shined her flashlight directly at Cameron.

"We're trying to go to sleep," said Logan.

"Hey, who's stopping you?"

"You are," said Logan.

"I'm just on my way out," he said.

"Where are you going at this time of night?" asked Gabby.

"Hate to break it to you girls, but it's only ten-fifteen," he replied. "I'm meeting some of the counselors in town. I mean, it *is* Saturday night."

"Cool," said Penny.

Cool? Once Cameron was out of earshot, she laughed because she knew she was a total dork. But she was starting to realize that all the girls were "dorks" here, in the same way that they were all "slutty." As Logan said, labels at camp—for better or worse—meant nothing. Penny was comforted by the realization that she was in good, if not decidedly dorky, company.

"Oh my God, you guys!" yelled Missy.

"What?"

"What's wrong?"

"Isn't it weird that . . ."

"That you're slutty?"

"No! I've known that for a while. But we didn't even realize that it's Saturday night! Isn't that so weird?"

"Every night is Saturday night at camp."

"Yeah, but it's different . . . I mean, think about it: what would you be doing right now if it was a Saturday night and you were at home?"

"Well, Worthe would be throwing a party at her parents' phat pad and probably getting her maid to drain the raspberry wine cooler out of the Steinway."

"How do they never catch you?"

"Easy: they're never there, they don't care . . . and, I pay off the doormen."

"Wow," said Penny, quickly putting her hand over her mouth as she anticipated Logan's glare. "Sorry."

"What would *you* be doing, Penny?" asked Logan.

"I don't know. Studying vocab words for the 'standardized test that shall not be named'? Maybe going to a movie?"

"Scintillating. Do we have to guess what Missy would be doing?"

"My boyfriend and I would be watching a movie and snuggling."

"Just snuggling?"

"He loves to snuggle!"

"Do any guys actually love to snuggle?"

"Sure! Lots of guys love to snuggle."

"Lo-Wo, if you weren't partying it up, you would probably be on some fabulous date with some fabulous high school God."

"Probably," replied Logan. "But it wouldn't be as much fun as this."

"Yeah, right!"

"Okay, it would be a different kind of fun. I bet Willow would be just across Central Park from me having an espresso at some Upper West Side coffee shop with her parents after having heard Freud speak."

"Freud is dead."

"I know that Freud is dead, Willow. I was being sarcastic."

"It's the only way my parents know how to relate to me . . . and to each other. Through psychological theories and ideology . . ."

"At least they try to relate to you."

"Yeah, my parents still treat me like I'm a child."

"My parents don't talk to each other."

"My mom is so annoying sometimes."

"I think my parents are afraid of understanding me."

"I kind of like my parents," said Penny.

"Well, bully for you," said Logan.

"Can I ask you guys a question?" asked Penny.

"No," said Logan.

"Logan!" yelled Willow.

"Seriously, rude much Logan?" asked Gabby.

"What?" asked Logan. "I just looooaaaaathe it when people say 'can I ask you a question?' It's like, hello, you just did! If you must *ask* if you can ask a question, then just say, 'can I ask two questions?' That would at least make more logical sense."

"What's your question, Penny?" asked Tess.

"What is it you guys love so much about camp?"

"Do you have eight weeks?"

"Um, actually I do."

"No you don't," muttered Logan.

"What I mean is, you all have lives and boyfriends and parties and everything back home, and . . . I don't really. Don't you miss the boys? Don't you miss parties and stuff? I mean, we're sixteen!"

"Are you kidding? It's such a relief to come back here! There's so much pressure . . . social pressure, academic pressure . . . and then we come here and we can just have fun in the exact same way we did when we were eight and it was still okay to be a kid."

"We don't have to put on makeup or do our hair or worry about our clothes."

"All we have to do is be ourselves."

"And embrace our inner dorkiness."

"Anyway, if I wasn't here," said Gabby, "I would probably be sitting at home alone with a pint of ice cream waiting for some boy of the moment to call me."

"Wah-wah!"

"It's true!"

"Gabby, I think you didn't get the memo: you're beautiful."

"I'm big."

"Big is beautiful."

"Are you agreeing I'm big?"

"Hey, you guys, I'm tired. And Gabby, you're not big," said Tess.

"Do you think any of us has rabies?"

"I hope not. That would really suck."

"Yeah, the last thing I need is to be foaming at the mouth all the time."

"Happy Saturday night, everyone!"

"I wouldn't want to be anywhere else!"

The girls cheered in agreement, and slowly quieted down as they fell asleep. Penny smiled. Is it possible that she didn't want to be anywhere else either?

The girls were awakened before reveille the next morning by Annie, who came back early from her day off to escort Bunk One to Portland for rabies shots—just as a precaution.

"Road trip!" yelled Missy.

"Rabies!" yelled Jade.

During the ride, the girls came up with new cheers:

"I have rabies, you have rabies, we have rabies all.
And when we get together, we do that rabies call:
Ee ee ee ee."

But what wasn't so funny was waiting in the emergency room all morning, and then finally getting the rabies shots, which were big and scary and painful. What's more, the shots were measured by the weight of the patient (that is, the bigger the girl, the bigger the shot). Gabby had to have the biggest shot, which depressed her to no end. So much so, that she even refused to get anything when they stopped at Dunkin' Donuts on the way back to camp (although she did take a bite of Penny's).

While Bunk One was away from camp, an exterminator had evicted "Freebird." The girls were relieved to be back and excited to have wild new stories to share with the rest of the camp. They even managed to have enough energy at dinner to make up more cheers. Jade put her arms out like wings, and the other girls followed. Annie nudged Penny so that she would know to do it, too. Dirk the Jerk was ensconced in trying to cut his rubbery mystery meat of the evening, and didn't notice that he had been targeted as the last one to copy their arm gestures until the girls shouted:

"Who's a bat? Who's a bat?
Who's a big fat rabies bat? Dirrrrrrrrrrk!!!"

"Was that supposed to be funny? I don't see how that's funny."

"You suck, Dirk," said Jade.

"What did you say?" he asked.

"Could you pass the duck, Dirk?"

"Is that what this is? I love duck!" he said.

"You're a quack," said Penny.

"What?"

"A duck says quack."

Just then, some of the girls at the next table yelled:

"Let's all cheer Bunk One, for not having rabies!
Sis boomedy hoo rah, Bunk One!"

Stacy stood up and shushed the dining hall.

"Welcome back, Bunk One. We're all thrilled you don't have rabies. As most of you know, tonight is the talent show. Please report to UTC right after dinner. Please do not dillydally . . . we have a lot of talented . . . and anxious . . . Fern Lake ladies who need to perform. You are dismissed!"

* * *

The talent show that night was an interesting combination of girls who were incredibly talented and those who were confident in their abilities but shockingly untalented, unco-ordinated, and/or tone-deaf. One girl played a beautiful and intricate Mozart piece on the piano. Another girl did a dance that was part ballet and part hip-hop (which, as far as Penny could tell, was quite good). Penny was happy to see that Morgan took part in the talent show by singing "Somewhere over the Rainbow." She was a little off-key, and the stage lights reflected off her thick glasses, which blinded the audience, but she sang with a lot of heart.

"Hey, Worthe, she's playing your song!" said Jade.

"Rainbow runs!"

"That's so hilarious, I forgot to laugh," said Logan.

And then there were the disasters: the two young girls who got up and played a duet of chopsticks on the piano and couldn't seem to get even that right; the girl who sang "Oops I Did It Again" a capella and then forgot the words and ran offstage crying; the girls who got onstage, were immediately overwhelmed by a fatal attack of the giggles, and ran off laughing without finishing (or starting, for that matter). And finally, there were the girls who tried to break-dance and just ended up banging into each other. It was funny until their heads started bleeding in the middle of the Centipede.

But the campers weren't nearly as funny as the counselors who followed. The Sailing Twins sang Céline Dion (with zero sense of irony). Annie and some of the other "cool" female counselors dressed up like male counselors and did a skit. Jerk Tennis did some weird and incredibly long jig with furious and alarming intensity. Water Rover Glenn sat on the side of the stage and accompanied himself on his guitar while he sang an earnest rendition of Cat Stevens's "Father and Son." A tear rolled down his cheek perfectly timed with the last note of the song.

"Oh, for the love of everything that is holy on this earth," said Jade.

"I know, isn't it nice?" asked Willow.

"Yeah, right. The *nicest*," said Jade.

When the talent show was over, the girls filed out of UTC. They were in their pajamas and UGG boots and slippers, and clutched their flashlights to guide them back to their bunks. They quietly critiqued the acts as they walked.

"And what about Dirk the Jerk's jig?"

"Try saying that five times!"

"Dirk the Jerk's jig Dirk the Jerk's jig Dirk the Gerk's gig Dirk dadirkdadig ig dirkjagig."

"I was kidding, Gabby, but nice work on that anyway."

"It's hard to do!"

"You know he totally thought it was genius!"

"Totally!"

The campus was filled with tired girls in pajamas shining their flashlights indiscriminately, slowly making their way back to their bunks. Penny liked these late-night walks. It was dark and it was quiet, but she never really knew what time it was at camp. It could have been 9 P.M., or it could have been four in the morning. Time was of no consequence there.

Penny was enjoying the assurance of at least one cookie at cookie line every day. And she was surprised to find that not only was she learning the cheers, but she also was actually enjoying knowing them and yelling them along with everyone else. She wasn't even sore from all the sports she was playing: softball, soccer, basketball, field hockey, and lacrosse (she played goalie and had come to love trudging across the field in full padding while the girls cheered).

Penny was finding the dependable camp routine to be both comforting and liberating: one bell told you to wake up, another to eat, another bell to change activities, and finally taps for lights-out and to tell you to go to sleep.

Now, if only there was a bell to make Logan Worthe like Penny Moore.

CAMP RULE #13

Fern Lake ladies never
ever get rowdy. R-O-W-D-Y.
Not even a little bit.

The girls were lying around Bunk One at rest hour, trying to write an original camp song, but they couldn't even agree on a tune to put it to.

"What about 'Welcome to the Jungle' by Guns n' Roses?" asked Missy.

"Yeah, not so much," said Jade.

"'Like a Virgin'?" asked Missy.

"Seriously, Missy, we need a song," said Willow. "How about something by the Beatles?"

"Come on, everybody does the Beatles or John Denver, let's think of something original," said Logan.

"No Dave Matthews! That guy is the frat boy answer to the Anti-Christ," said Jade.

"I love Dave Matthews."

"Of course you do."

"I'm bored. Penny had a great idea for a prank," said Logan.

"I did?" Penny asked.

Logan stared her down.

"I did!" said Penny.

"Like David Hasselhoff-bad?"

"Did I hear someone say 'prank'?" asked Gabby.

"Did I hear someone say David Hasselhoff?" asked Missy. "Maybe it's my German heritage, but there's just something about that guy that makes me want to drown myself so that he'll come save me and then serenade me on the beach after resuscitating me . . . with tongue."

"That is scarily well thought out," said Penny.

"Penny was talking about Dirk the Jerk," said Logan. "She thinks he needs a secret admirer."

"I like it," said Jade.

"Penny the rule breaker strikes again!"

"*Great* idea, Penny!"

"Thanks," she said. She was still disturbed by Missy's David Hasselhoff fantasy.

"Who has good handwriting?" asked Logan.

"I do!" said Tess.

"Okay, write this down," said Missy. As she cleared her throat dramatically, Jade jumped in.

"Dear Jerk . . ."

"You can't call him Jerk in a love letter!"

"You're right. Dear Dirk, your loins . . . ," started Missy.

"Loins?" asked Jade.

"What's wrong with loins?"

"She's right," said Penny. "It's just so 'on the nose.'"

"What's wrong with her nose?" asked Gabby.

"Is a nose considered to be a loin?"

"Okay, let's focus, people!" said Logan.

"Okay. Dear Dirk," said Gabby.

"I have been watching you," said Jade.

"Ew! Creeeeeeeeeeepy!" said Missy.

"We need like, imagery, and stuff."

"And metaphors."

"And rhymes."

"Hey, guys, it was Penny's idea. Why don't you try it, Penny?" asked Logan.

"But . . ."

"Dig deep," said Logan. "Pretend it's Cameron."

"Oh no she di'int!" said Gabby.

"Who are you?" asked Jade.

"I'm Gabby."

"You're a freak."

"*You're* a freak."

"Let your freak flag fly!"

"Dear Dirk . . . ," started Penny.

"Here she goes!"

"Woop, there it is!"

"Seriously, Gabby, stop."

"When I look at you . . ."

Penny couldn't say just how it happened, but the poetry started flowing out of her. She spent the remainder of rest hour dictating a secret admirer note to Dirk the Jerk. And with a few tweaks and suggestions, the final product was a masterpiece.

"Dear Dirk,
When I look at you,
I don't know what to do.
Because you are such an Adonis of a man,
I can't help but be your biggest fan.
Your lips are like plump melons,
And by stealing my heart,
You could be considered a felon.
Love,
Your secret admirer"

The girls decided to leave it in his mailbox before dinner that evening. The whole experience made them so excited that they did more cheers during the meal than usual, including Penny's new favorite . . . which she actually started!

"Let's get a little bit rowdy: R-O-W-D-Y."

After the final *Y*, they would stomp their feet. They repeated this over and over, getting louder each time as more girls joined in until the whole dining room was yelling and stomping and definitely getting rowdy.

Penny noticed that Tess was phoning in her rowdiness, and not stomping at all. She was never the loudest girl in the group, but tonight she was inordinately quiet. Penny could have sworn that Tess winced as she got up from the table. When she limped to the door, Penny followed her.

"Are you okay?" asked Penny.

"Yes. I'm fine."

"You're limping, Tess."

"No, I'm not."

"Yeah, you are."

"Okay, listen. My ankle is hurting. A little. I twisted it today. Don't tell anyone, okay? I'm sure it'll be fine."

"Tess, you have to go get that looked at. You could make it worse."

"I'm fine. Besides, I can't miss a day of training. My parents will kill me."

"Who cares? They wouldn't want you to be in pain or injured."

"I'm fine."

"What's wrong?" asked Willow.

"Tess hurt herself," said Penny.

"Here we go," said Tess.

"Tess hurt herself?" asked Gabby.

"What?"

"What happened?"

"In the bunk, girls. Now," said Logan.

"Nice work," said Tess. She scowled at Penny.

Logan and the girls forced Tess to tell them about her ankle, and they made her promise she would go to the infirmary the next day.

"Let's do something to cheer you up," said Penny.

"That's a great idea!" said Gabby. "We could braid one another's hair and play jacks!"

"Hey, Gabby, wake up and smell your age, would you? We're not *four*," said Jade.

"I love jacks," mumbled Gabby.

"You guys, really, I'm fine," said Tess.

"Can it, Tessie," said Jade. She and Logan then went into their own cheer:

> *"I'm a martyr, you're a martyr, we are martyrs all,*
> *And when we get together, we do our martyr call,*
> *'I'm fiiiiiiiiiiiiiiiiiiiiiine!'"*

"Wah-waaaaah."

"Logan, maybe you could use the lightbulb string as a noose to hang Willow's stuffed horse again?"

"I can't believe you guys remember that! That was like a hundred summers ago."

"It was last summer."

"It was all in good fun."

"Yup, nothing says good times like a beloved stuffed horse hung by its neck from a lightbulb."

"Hey, at least I didn't make the poor horse look like he was masturbating . . . um, Missy!!!"

"Masturbation is a natural thing! Birds do it, bees do it . . . even stuffed horses do it!"

"Okay, we'll get back to the masturbation topic later," said Logan. "Let's focus, girls. Remember those ice cream sundaes we had for dessert tonight?"

"Do I ever," said Gabby. "I think I just hiccupped a little of it up a minute ago."

"Gross," said Jade.

"T.M.I," said Missy.

"The point is, girls, Penny had a great idea, which she shared with me earlier and I think she should share it with the group."

"I did?"

Logan raised her eyebrows and nodded. Penny shrugged. She had no idea what Logan was talking about. Logan became visibly frustrated.

"I did!" said Penny.

"Penny was saying that she bet there's more where those sundaes came from," said Logan.

"Right. That's what I was saying," stammered Penny.

"You mean, the kitchen?" asked Missy.

"No, the greenie," said Jade. "Yes, of course the kitchen! Love your work, Moore."

"But we can't sneak in! If we get caught, we'll lose canteen for a week!" said Gabby.

"Canteen-shmanteen," said Logan.

"But seriously, what if we get caught?" asked Missy.

"Yeah, rule-breaker-Penny, what if we get caught?"

Logan and Penny locked eyes.

"We won't get caught," said Logan. "Penny never gets caught."

"Logan, could you come here for a minute please?"

"The rule breaker wants to talk to little old me? Sure! Let's go to my office."

Penny and Logan went out the back door of the bunk and into the "greenie," which Penny guessed temporarily functioned as Logan's "office."

"Logan, isn't this, like, vandalism or trespassing or something majorly bad?"

"Trespassing-shmespassing, vandalism-shmandalism . . ."

"Okay, you have to stop doing that."

"Look, I'm not saying we're going to get caught, but

if we did, we'll just say you suggested it. See, Moore, you won't have to do anything technically illegal and we'll all be along with you for the ride. And you get a sundae, too! I mean, what's better than that? You do still want to get out of here, don't you?"

"Oh. Yeah. Totally," said Penny, lying.

"So, then, this is your moment," said Logan. "You make the choice: do you want to be remembered as a leader or as a follower?"

Logan unlatched the door, grabbed Penny's hand, and pulled her into the bunk.

"Okay," said Penny. "Let's get it together, people. Operation Ice Cream Sundae is in full effect! We're going for grim reaper garb: that means everyone in black ASAP!"

The girls laughed and cheered, but Penny's emotions were mixed. On one hand, she loved the idea of a mission, and of doing something wild . . . and of being the leader of it. She also really wanted to cheer up Tess, and felt badly that she had betrayed her confidence by telling the rest of the girls, even though she truly felt it was the right thing to do. And now here she was, leading Bunk One on a covert night mission into the Fern Lake Camp kitchen.

They waited until after midnight, when they saw the last of the kitchen staff leave for the night. They tiptoed in single file, giggling and shushing one another the whole way. Tess put one arm around Penny, and the other around

Gabby for support so that she could keep up with the group despite her gimp ankle.

"Thank you, Penny," Tess whispered.

"I'm just here to help," said Penny.

"I'm glad you're here."

"Thanks."

Jade shined her flashlight on the front screen door of the kitchen and tried to pull it open. But it wouldn't budge. She pulled again. She put her left foot up on the wall next to the door and leaned back, pulling it with all her weight.

"It's locked!" said Jade.

"Since when do they lock the kitchen?" asked Gabby.

"Since Paxton got in there one night last summer and coated himself with chocolate sauce, marshmallows, and graham crackers," said Logan.

"Why would he do that?" asked Penny.

"He wanted to become a human s'more."

"Hey, Penny, you haven't been to camp before. Have you ever had a s'more?" asked Gabby.

"Sure. Totally. I like s'mores," said Penny.

The girls stopped in their tracks.

"Um, you *like* s'mores? Nobody just *likes* s'mores."

"Unless somebody has never had a really truly Fern Lake lady-made s'more."

"Afraid not."

"Okay, hello?" hissed Logan. "Let's deal with Penny's

s'more deprivation another time please. We have a kitchen crisis here."

"Well, does anyone have, like, a ratchet or something?" asked Gabby.

"What are you talking about?" asked Jade.

"A ratchet! It just sounds like something that could cut a lock, don't you think?"

"Over here! The window!" said Missy.

They quickly tiptoed over to where Missy was standing. There was a small open window that was about ten feet off the ground.

"Too bad none of us can reach it," said Penny. And then before any of the girls could say it first, Penny declared the requisite "WAH-WAAAAH."

The girls laughed and started quietly chanting, "Downer, downer, downer!"

"Hey, guys," interrupted Jade. "Do you remember the bunk picture we took two summers ago?"

"Human pyramid!" they yelled in unison.

"Oh no," said Willow.

"Come on, Willow, you're the smallest!"

"And the most agile!"

"Take one for the team, would you?"

"Not the human pyramid . . . not again!"

"Come on, Willow. Do it for Tess. Do you see how sad and hungry she is?"

"Feed me," said Tess, quietly.

The girls created a human pyramid, with Logan, Jade, and Gabby on their hands and knees forming the bottom tier, Penny and Missy on top of them forming the second tier, and then Tess helped Willow climb over the girls to get to the top.

"Ow!"

"Watch it!"

"That's my hand!"

"My hair is caught in your lanyard!"

"Your knee is piercing my spleen!"

"Your spleen is on the other side of your body, nimrod."

"It's all fun and games until someone loses an ovary!"

"Okay, I'm ready," said Willow.

"Finally!"

"Okay, girls: one, two, three, jump, Willow!"

"Jump! Jump like the wind, Willow! Jump like the wind!"

And with that, Willow disappeared through the window, landing just a moment later with a loud thud.

"Willow? You okay?"

"I fell on my skull!" she yelled from inside the kitchen.

"Wah-wah."

"Ding ding!" said Willow.

The girls ran to the front of the kitchen just as Willow opened the door with an ice cream sandwich balanced on her head where a small bump was already forming.

"Welcome to paradise, girls," said Logan.

The girls filed in quickly and quietly, and made a bee-line for the freezer. The Bunk One girls, having spent the last four zillion summers together at FLC, were no strangers to the Fern Lake kitchen.

"One night every summer, we are granted 'Kitchen Permission,'" said Willow.

"K.P.!" the girls whispered.

"So, this would be an unauthorized K.P.?"

"Exactly."

"So what happens during a legal K.P.?"

"We have an hour to make and eat as much cinnamon toast as camper-ly possible," said Jade.

"Gabby holds the record for most slices eaten in one sitting."

"I'm proud . . . and ashamed of it," said Gabby.

"She's conflicted," said Willow.

"It's true," said Gabby. "But right now, I am literally drooling with excitement."

It took two girls to pull out each heavy tub of ice cream. They grabbed bottles of chocolate sauce and sprinkles. They even found some mushy bananas to make banana splits. Tess ate a spoonful from her huge bowl of ice cream with all the toppings.

"I can't remember the last time I had a bowl of ice cream."

"Tessie, it's all about moderation," said Willow.

"I don't know, Will. Moderation always seemed so extreme to me," said Logan, spraying the Reddi-wip directly into her mouth.

"I would never do this at home," said Gabby.

"Gab, when I stayed at your house that weekend over the winter, we went through like two pints of Ben & Jerry's," said Missy.

"Well, almost never."

They giggled and "wah-wahed" and ate as much ice cream as they could. But whether it was the sugar high or the heat of the camp kitchen, or a little bit of both, Penny decided to take the whole experience to the next level. She held up a spoonful of chocolate ice cream, and aimed it directly at Logan.

"Pennnnnnnnnnny . . . ," warned Willow.

Logan looked up to see the ice cream aimed at her forehead. She looked directly at Penny.

"The hunter has become the hunted," said Penny.

The other girls giggled. Logan put her spoon down and looked at Penny squarely.

"I dare you," she said.

The old Penny would always have chosen truth over dare, or would have shied away from the game and the girls altogether. But this was the new Penny, the Camp Penny, and Camp Penny left no dare untaken. She catapulted the chocolate ice cream at Logan's face. It landed on her right eye, which she had closed just in time. Logan sat quietly with her eyes closed while the ice cream slowly slid down her cheek, landing with an audible "plop" on her black sweatshirt. She looked down at the ice cream blob, and then back at Penny. Logan started to smile, but it wasn't the fake Mc-smile Penny had seen that first night at dinner. No, this smile was genuine, determined, maybe even intrigued.

"You are so dead, Moore," said Logan.

With lightning speed, Logan grabbed the entire economy-size bottle of chocolate sauce with one hand and the collar of Penny's shirt with the other. She squeezed the bottle as it ran down Penny's chest. As if on cue, Gabby sprayed Missy with whipped cream.

"You guys!" started Willow. "Seriously, you guys, this is really . . . we probably shouldn't . . . it's very puerile behavior!"

At which point, Logan and Penny—together—took the rest of the now lukewarm vat of ice cream and put the entire thing over Willow's head. Through the cardboard and ice cream, Willow said:

"All right, this is war."

"I thought you were a pacifist!"

"Pacifism has no place in a . . ."

"Food fight!" they yelled.

And that's when everyone joined in. They threw, sprayed, and smothered everything foodlike they could find until they were covered from the top of their heads to the tips of their toes in some form of sugar. And then they were suddenly blinded by an excessively bright beam of light. The girls froze, covered in the evidence.

"Ladies! Ladies! What do you think you're doing?"

Penny recognized the voice immediately. It was unmistakable. It was Stacy. The girls looked at one another nervously. Gabby started to sing Stacy's song.

"Her name is Stacy, we love her so much it's—"

"Can it!" said Stacy. "Whose idea was this? Speak up! Hm—I've never heard you girls so quiet before! If no one steps forward, you will all suffer the consequences."

The girls looked down at their feet. Penny caught Logan's ice-cream-soaked eye, and then Logan turned away. Covered in every sundae-related substance, Penny stepped forward. She swallowed, hard. This was it. This was how she was going to go down. She started to think about how they would find her duffels among all the others, and about how her parents would feel when they got the phone call that their sweet daughter had been kicked out of camp. Would they be disappointed in her? Of course they would be! Would the camp tell Penny's school? What would she do with the rest of her summer? The time had come. Everyone was staring at Penny. She opened her mouth to speak.

"I will ask you one more time," said Stacy, "whose idea was this?"

"It was—" started Penny.

"It was . . . everyone's idea," said Tess, limping forward.

"What?" asked Logan.

"I hurt myself and the whole bunk was trying to cheer me up."

"I don't buy it," said Stacy.

"It's true," said Gabby. She kicked Tess in the ankle.

"Ow! What's wrong with you?"

"I was just showing Stacy that you're hurt?"

"By crippling me?"

"It's not anyone's fault," said Missy.

"If you ask me, I think we still have some rabies," said Gabby.

"Yeah, look, Gabby's still foaming at the mouth!"

"I am not! I mean, okay, I am."

"Something's going on here. And I don't like it. I don't like it one little itsy-bitsy teeny-weeny bit. Not at all. No, sir. I'm watching you, Moore," said Stacy. "Now, clean this up pronto and return to your bunk. You will report to George's office tomorrow."

Stacy quickly turned and walked out of the kitchen.

"Woohoo!" yelled Jade.

"Thank you, guys," said Tess. "This was the best cheer-up mission ever."

"I can't believe you guys stuck up for me," said Penny. "I was ready to give myself up. Thank you, Bunk One."

"Yeah, why did you guys do that?" asked Logan. "It was Penny's idea after all!"

"Hey, Logan, whatever happened to all for Bunk One and Bunk One for all?"

"That went out the window when we got a new girl in our bunk for what was supposed to be our last and best year!"

"Logan, Penny is one of us now," said Tess.

"Oh, really?" asked Logan. "Well that's just great. That's just fan-friggin-tastic. So you're choosing the new girl over me, your friend and bunk mate of eight summers? That's nice. That's rich. That is reeeeally rich."

"Logan, we are not choosing Penny over you. It's not a competition."

"Everything is a competition! Life is a competition!"

"Well, camp isn't life. Did you forget that? This is Fern Lake, not Lakefield Academy. And you're not the ruler of the Fab Four here, Logan. Here, you're just one of us, the way you've always been. For better or worse."

"Fine, if that's how you all feel. Then the tribe has spoken."

Logan walked out of the kitchen.

"You know she's pissed when she starts using reality show jargon. This is not good."

"I'm sorry, you guys. I didn't mean for this to happen, you know."

"We know, Penny."

"Let's just start cleaning up. We've got a lot of work to do."

The girls looked around the kitchen, which was covered with a thick film of ice cream. Jade started handing out the mops, and all the girls—minus Logan—started cleaning up.

CAMP RULE #14

Fern Lake ladies do not dare counselors to eat or drink things that will make them vomit.

The *good news* was that Tess's ankle was just twisted, not broken. The bad news was that she couldn't play tennis (or any sports for that matter) for two weeks. Apparently, her parents did not take it well. Tess, however, had quickly gotten over it by spending a double period in arts and crafts.

Logan, on the other hand, had remained alarmingly quiet since the Sundae Mission, and didn't seem to be engaging anyone in Bunk One.

Bunk One got a smack-down from George, who took away their candy canteen for the rest of the summer (which, because this was their last summer, was effectively taking away canteen for the rest of their lives)! But as Willow said, "They would always have the fond memory of Mission: Ice Cream Sundae," and no one could take *that* away.

Because it was raining (requisite wah-wah), the scheduled hot dog and hamburger cookout had to be held in the dining room. Gabby dropped her fork while talking animatedly and gesticulating wildly to Annie, attempting to describe the late-night food fight. When she came back up from retrieving it under the table, she was bright red. She whispered to Tess, who also turned red, and then Tess "dropped" her fork and went under the table to get it. This happened over and over again, girl by girl, until Penny—out of order and curious as to what all the hubbub was about—decided to see for herself.

Nothing seemed amiss under the table . . . until Penny noticed Dirk the Jerk's lower half. Sure, he was wearing his uniform shorts. But he was not wearing anything underneath them! And he was definitely "hanging out." Dirk the Jerk was going commando, and it was totally gross! Penny bit her lip and came back up to the table. She looked at the other girls, and then at Dirk the Jerk. There was really only one thing to say, as far as she was concerned.

"Um, Dirk, could you please pass the wieners?" asked Penny.

The girls exploded with laughter. Even Logan laughed but then immediately hid it, and resumed scowling. Missy put her arm around Penny's shoulders, and they were both

crying because they were laughing so hard. Willow was trying not to laugh because "the human body is a beautiful and
natural thing," but even she couldn't seem to help herself.

This episode sparked renewed interest in the Jerk-love-
letter scheme. But it was Penny—independently of Logan—
who suggested that they take it up a notch. Logan sat out
this time, silently reading a book on her own bed. Penny
thought it was time for Dirk the Jerk to meet his admirers.
The next day was spent composing the second love letter.

> "Dearest Dirk,
> Your voice is like honey,
> How I would like to be the carrot to your bunny.
> I think of you and me and all we could be,
> So please meet me . . .
> Behind the bunks at the ropes course at
> Midnight tomorrow (Thursday/Friday).
> Love,
> Your secret admirer"

Penny was nominated to be the one to slip the note into
Dirk the Jerk's mailbox the next day before lunch because it
was "Penny's idea," and she was the "rule breaker." The girls
watched from around the corner of the dining room as Dirk
the Jerk went to his mailbox, took out the letter, and surrep-

titiously opened it. He read the note, looked up and around him (looking terribly paranoid and guilty), and then stuck it into the pocket of his white tennis shorts. He walked into the dining room—stick-straight, pseudononchalant—and past the girls as they plastered themselves on the wall behind the glass doors so that he couldn't see them.

"Ladies," said Paxton. He tipped his cowboy hat at the girls as he walked through the door to the dining room, making a beeline for his parents' table and the strawberry juice box that awaited him there.

After another semi-inedible camp meal, and several "dropped" forks—just to ensure that Dirk the Jerk was not going commando again—the girls did the usual disgusting cleanup. They dumped all remaining contents of each plate onto the stack of plates being passed back to the head of the table. The leftover liquids went into one container: milk, water, bug juice, and anything else that could be described as "not solid."

"You girls are so spoiled, you don't realize how lucky you are," said Dirk the Jerk. "Just look at all this food being wasted."

Logan and Penny locked eyes across the table. It was obvious they were having the same devious thought. Logan opened her mouth instinctively, but Penny took the lead and jumped in.

"Well, then, don't waste it!" said Penny. "Drink this!"

Penny slid the container of discarded liquids toward Dirk the Jerk. It overflowed a little onto the table. It was a brownish color and had particles of Willow's abandoned soy milk floating in it. Penny poured some of it into a fresh paper cup.

"Oh my God! That's like ninety-five percent backwash!" said Gabby.

"That could *kill* a person!" said Missy.

"No, it couldn't, you nimrod," said Jade.

"I would do it! Don't think I wouldn't do it. It's all-natural," said Dirk the Jerk.

"So, do it," said Penny.

The girls chanted: "Do it, do it, do it!"

"Bottoms up!" he said.

Dirk the Jerk held the cup up to the girls as if it were a toast. He maintained eye contact with them as he drank the entire thing in one shot. He confidently placed the cup down on the table with an accomplished tap. He winced a bit, shook his head, and burped.

"See?" he said smugly. "No problem!"

And then he vomited all over the linoleum floor.

The girls were laughing until Annie saw Dirk the Jerk's vomit, and she vomited, too—right on the table. As Annie's vomit started making its way across the table, the girls jumped back to avoid it, knocking over the bench they were sitting on in the process. They managed to escape just in time as Annie's vomit dripped off the edges of the table onto the floor. Penny couldn't breathe because she was laughing so hard (and simultaneously trying not to vomit).

"I just peed in my pants I'm laughing so hard!" said Missy.

"At least you didn't vomit in them!" said Penny.

Barb, George, and Stacy must have heard the benches crashing, because they rushed over to Table One. When they saw and smelled what was happening, Barb vomited on the floor, which splashed onto George's kneesocks, and then Stacy promptly vomited onto her clipboard.

"Cool!" said Paxton. "It's a bona fide barf-athon!"

"This is *not* cool, Paxton!" said Barb.

"Says you!"

Paxton reached into his pocket and took out a disposable camera with which he started taking pictures.

"Stop it, Paxton!" said George. "Bunk One, I want you in my office just as soon as you finish cleaning up this mess . . . and I change my socks."

The girls had to put their shirts over their mouths because the smell was so nauseating. Penny was learning never to put anything past a Fern Lake lady; even vomit. By the time they went to see George, his socks were indeed clean . . . and still pulled up to his knees. His office was filled with pictures of family, campers, trophies, and FLC artifacts. The girls sat on the two sofas while he remained behind his desk.

"Girls, I shouldn't need to tell you this, but you're supposed to be setting an example," he said. "You're in my office twice in one week! You girls were never this mischievous. I mean, sure Logan had that Flintstones vitamins incident years ago, but you girls are Fern Lake ladies! You're Bunk One!"

"You're right, George," said Logan. "I mean, we were never like this before. I wonder what's changed this year that might have affected our behavior? I can't think of anything because the only thing new this summer is . . . Penny."

Was Penny going to get kicked out of camp for having started a vomit fest? She didn't want to leave, but she tried desperately to look on the bright side and realized that the summer-camp-vomit-exit might make for a great (if not unique) college essay.

"Penny, are you responsible for this?"

"Yes, George, I am," she said. "I mean, I guess I am. I dared Jerk, I mean, Dirk to drink the liquid leftovers, but I had no idea he would puke from it."

"Penny, that's not how we do things here at Fern Lake Camp. We do not dare counselors to drink things that will make them vomit. Do I make myself clear?" he asked.

"Absolutely," said Penny, noticing just a speck of vomit on his sneakers. "It will never happen again."

"I would take away your canteen, but you girls already lost all canteen privileges for that kitchen stunt you pulled."

"You could send her home," said Logan.

"Logan!" said several of the girls at once.

"What?" asked Logan. "Jeez. It was just a thought."

"You are dismissed," said George.

The girls filed out and walked toward the bunk.

"What is wrong with you?" asked Jade.

"Nothing," said Logan. "Just . . . leave me alone."

"Yeah, Logan . . . seriously, you've gotta lighten up."

"And take it easier on Penny."

"Excuse me?"

"She's a lot of fun!"

"Can't we all just get along?" asked Willow.

"Yeah, this is such a waste of time in the promised land."

But Logan didn't answer, so the girls walked back to the bunk in silence.

CAMP RULE #15

For Fern Lake ladies, a bathing
suit is most certainly NOT optional.

After having been at Fern Lake Camp for over two weeks, Penny had tried every sport, every art shop, every meal . . . but she had not yet experienced the "Outdoor Living" department. Finally, Bunk One was scheduled for "O.L.," which, in addition to general camping tips, included a high ropes course.

Penny was already late, but she ran back to the bunk to change out of her sweaty soccer clothes and into long sweatpants. When Penny barreled in, Jade was alone in the bunk, sitting on her bed.

"Oh, hey," said Penny, almost out of breath.

"Hey."

"I just came back to change," said Penny.

"Hey, it's your bunk, too."

"It is, isn't it?" she said.

"Do you have any inner dialogue whatsoever?"

"Apparently not."

Penny changed as fast as she could and grabbed her bug spray.

"Are you coming to Outdoor Living? I mean, 'O.L.'?" Penny asked.

"You mean Poison Ivy Living—or, PIL?" asked Jade. "Eventually, I guess. I'm pretty busy right now picking at the scabs from my mosquito bites."

"Hm. Pleasant. Well, do you want me to wait for you?"

"Nah, probably not a good idea."

"Are you going to come at all?"

"Not sure. I'm weighing my options. If I go, I risk a full-on breakdown because of my fear of heights; if I stay here I get in trouble for cutting the activity. I have this quandary every summer."

"My mom is afraid of heights," said Penny.

"Oh yeah, so what does she do?"

"Well, she used to meditate. But now she just takes a Xanax."

"Yeah, my dad has those. If I were home, I could just go steal one if I wanted. He would never know. But that's what I like about camp. No temptations. It's nice. For the most part, I follow the rules here. Unlike you . . ."

"Well, if you follow the rules here, then maybe you should get going and give it another try?"

"Yeah, I guess. Although I've lost my canteen for the rest of my life anyway, so I'm not sure exactly what they could take away from me."

"Worse things could happen."

"Yeah, I could get kicked out."

Jade laughed, but Penny just stood there. She didn't even want to be late to her next activity, so how could she still want to leave camp altogether? Penny knew only two things at that moment: she wanted to try out this zip wire thing, and she didn't want Jade to have an anxiety attack.

Penny and Jade walked to the O.L. area in the woods behind the bunks. As the rest of Bunk One saw them coming, they immediately started cheering:

> *"Let's all cheer, Jade and Penny*
> *For gracing us with their presence.*
> *Sis boomedy hoorah, Jade, sis boomedy hoorah, Penny,*
> *Sis boomedy hoorah presence."*

The girls played trust games, and "learned about the outdoors," but it was the high ropes course that was supposedly the highlight of the day. The girls were strapped into harnesses and were "on belay," clipped into a support rope—even if they fell, they would be safe. But this did not seem to comfort Jade. She looked up at the zip wire, which was about fifty feet off the ground. The other girls seemed to love it, but apparently Jade had to be talked down every summer. It was the most vulnerable anyone ever saw her. Jade was in a cold sweat. Penny stayed on the platform with her until she was ready to go.

"You couldn't have just told them it was that time of the month the way Missy always does?" Penny suggested.

Jade laughed. And then she stopped abruptly and looked scared again.

"You don't have to, like, babysit me up here or anything," said Jade.

"I know," said Penny. "I just . . . I kind of like it up here. It's quiet, y'know?"

"Yeah, maybe if I ever get over my pathological fear of heights, I'll come up here just to ponder the meaning of life."

"Well, when you figure it out, will you let me know?"

"Yeah, sure."

"So, you ready?"

"Come on, Jade!" yelled Gabby from the safety of terra firma.

"You're the wind beneath my wings!" yelled Tess.

"Don't you ever quote Bette Midler to me again!" yelled Jade.

"Bette Midler could get down that zip wire faster," said Missy.

"Hey, calm your hormones, slutface!"

"They've been calming for forty minutes already!" said Missy.

Jade closed her eyes and took a deep breath.

"You can do it, Jade," whispered Penny.

Jade looked straight ahead. She closed her eyes, clenched her teeth, and then jumped off the platform. She flew down the zip wire screaming bloody murder the whole way. When she got to the bottom, the girls hugged her, and helped her open the carabineer that connected her harness to the zip wire.

Penny watched from the platform where she stood, attached but alone. She was at the same height as the top of the trees that surrounded her. At that moment, she may not have been contemplating the meaning of life, but she may very well have been contemplating the meaning of camp. And it meant that she was truly happy.

"Hoorah hoorah hoorah, Penny!" the girls yelled.

"Sis boom bah, Bunk One rah!" Penny replied.

She took a deep breath, jumped off the platform, zipped down the wire, and enjoyed every exhilarating moment of it. Penny may have been "zipping" down, but it felt like she was moving in slow motion as she descended from the tree-tops, flying gracefully and effortlessly, her hair and her FLC uniform blowing in the summer breeze. She could see Bunk One ahead, cheering for her, their voices getting louder and their smiling faces becoming more discernible as she came closer to them. For Penny, for just a moment, everything was perfect. She was perfect, Bunk One was perfect, camp was perfect. Now, if only she didn't have the worst wedgie of all time. *Wah-wah.*

After lights-out that night, the girls staked out the ropes course in hopes of seeing Dirk the Jerk's reaction upon finding the last secret admirer note they had left for him. They had even created elaborate directional and warning signals. Of course, they forgot which ones meant what, so they kept bumping into one another and scaring one another in the dark. Tess stayed on lookout, as she couldn't move very fast with her bad ankle, and they were afraid they might need to retreat from the scene in a hurry. But Dirk the Jerk was nowhere to be seen, and the girls were easily creeped out by the woods and bored with waiting, so they retreated back to Bunk One.

Gabby's parents had hidden a bag of Triscuits and a can of cheddar Easy Cheese—which the girls insisted on calling "Squeeze Cheese"—in a green-colored stuffed animal of indeterminate species, and they were eager to start eating.

"God, there is absolutely nothing I love more than squeezing cheese from a can," said Gabby.

"And look at the pretty designs I can make with it on my Triscuit!" said Tess.

"See, it's creative *and* delicious! It's the wonder food!" said Gabby.

It was a veritable processed food feast in Bunk One that night. The girls sat together in the middle of the bunk: some of them leaning against their beds, some against their cubbies, some lying on their stomachs on the hard, wood floor. They were chowing on Triscuits, Wheat Thins, Squeeze Cheese, all the Crystal Light pink lemonade they could drink, and many, *many* pistachio nuts (Missy's mother had smuggled a pound of pistachios in the bottom of a spa kit she sent). Willow offered everyone the all-natural vegan sesame candies that *her* mother had sent, but everyone politely declined (and that was even before they realized that Willow's mother had hidden the candies in a potpourri pillow, so they smelled more like lavender than anything edible).

When the girls woke up the next morning, empty cans and stray pistachio shells littered the floor. Missy almost cut her foot on them before running over to the ropes course to see that the note for Dirk the Jerk . . . was gone.

Their one day in Outdoor Living had been to prepare Bunk One for their overnight, scheduled for a few days later. The overnight was just on the beach at the Fern Lake waterfront, but it was a treat because the girls got to camp out and have a big campfire.

They sang songs, cheered, and talked about funny things

that had happened B.P.: Before Penny. Just a few weeks ago, these stories would have made Penny feel left out and unwanted, but now she was actually enjoying them. And, for what it was worth, it seemed like the girls were enjoying having a captive audience—everyone except Logan, who seemed to be getting more sullen by the day. The girls did their best to include her, and ignore her Debbie Downer vibe at the same time. Penny felt guilty that Logan was so miserable and that, unintentionally, Penny was the cause of it. But, honestly, Logan was acting like a brat. She had never even given Penny a chance. Whether Logan liked it or not, the Bunk One girls seemed to actually like Penny. Well, they liked the camp-rule-breaker-enhanced Penny, but they liked Penny nonetheless, and Penny felt she had a right to enjoy that.

"So, we were on *Olympia*," started Jade.

"Wait, what's *Olympia*?" asked Penny.

"It's the name of this old-school motorboat with a red-and-white-striped awning. One night each summer, every bunk got to go out on it. It had a little barbecue attached to it, so we used to make s'mores . . ."

"'Used to' being the key phrase."

"Why? What happened?"

"Well, genius here was on like her hundredth s'more . . ."

"It was my third!" said Gabby.

"Whatever."

"And she was conducting with her stick o' flaming marshmallows as Missy sang her haftorah portion from her bat mitzvah."

"It was very good, by the way," said Willow.

"Thank you. Did I tell you my Hebrew tutor had no ankles?"

"We know," said Jade.

"No ankles?"

"Kankles."

"Okay . . ."

"And Gabby became so passionate about her conducting that she set the roof of *Olympia* on fire."

"The roof! The roof! The roof is on fire!" sang Missy.

"Thank you, Missy, for that vocal interlude," said Jade.

"And so we started screaming, 'Drop and roll! Drop and roll!'" said Willow.

"So she did . . . and she ended up getting burnt marshmallow in her hair. We had to cut it all off."

"It was not my best look."

"It was very gamine," said Willow.

"*Gamine* is not a term used to describe a Jewish girl with singed and frizzy hair that has been cut unevenly by all her bunk mates."

"Wah-waaaaaaaah!"

"Meanwhile, Jade is screaming 'iceberg, straight ahead!'

while Willow was trying to fan the flames with her *paper* fan which *obviously* caught on fire."

"I loved that fan," lamented Willow.

"So, we're on the 'burning boat,' Gabby is rolling around in melted marshmallow, Jade is yelling, Missy was blowing on the fire while Willow was fanning the flames and Tess was hurling soda into it, and finally Mike put the fire out with a jug of water."

"And where were you, Logan?" asked Penny.

"Oh, Logan jumped ship and was halfway back to camp," said Missy.

"Yeah, way to take one for the team, Lo-Wo," said Jade.

"I was going back to get help, if you must know!" Logan piped in.

"Yeah, right."

Penny was laughing so hard by the time the girls had finished telling the story that she actually had to catch her breath. She tried to drink some pink lemonade from her canteen, but the girls kept laughing, and it ended up coming out through her nose, which only made everyone laugh more.

"Oh my God!" cried Missy. "I totally just peed in my pants."

"What else is new?"

"Missy always pees in her pants when she laughs too hard."

"Some girls write home to have their parents send candy, Missy writes home to have her parents send Depends."

"I have a weak bladder!" yelled Missy.

"Come on, sweet thing, you know we love you."

"Yeah, you know ur-ine our hearts always," said Logan.

"And she's back, ladies and gentlemen!" said Jade. "Thank you, Logan, for that quick yet oh-so-nostalgic trip back to the Catskills. We're happy you stopped by!"

"I couldn't resist," said Logan quietly.

The girls jumped up and piled on top of her.

"We love you, Lo-Wo!"

"We always love you!"

"Even when you're a stubborn brat!"

Penny remained at the campfire, alone, watching the pileup. She desperately wanted to be a part of it. But it didn't seem like Logan was ever going to let that happen. Maybe Logan was right. Maybe it *was* a competition after all?

The girls pitched their tents as they had learned to do. They ate mac and cheese, and some soggy iceberg lettuce, and canned beans (and then played several rounds of "not it" as to who was going to sleep in a tent with Gabby). They ate out of their steel mess kits, and then washed them in the lake, which Penny found to be more than slightly sketchy and unsanitary. But, when in camp!

Willow gathered the sticks for everyone to roast their marshmallows. Gabby, the self-described s'more connoisseur/consultant, took Penny through the process of creating the universe's most perfect s'more. Apparently, the key factor was the roasting of the marshmallow: it was essential that it was *browned*, not burned. Gabby pointed to Jade and Logan—who had zero patience—as the example of what *not* to do. They thrust their marshmallows in the fire, setting them immediately aflame. They then stuck the flaming marshmallows between two graham crackers and blocks of Hershey's chocolate. Jade's cracker broke, so she shoved the whole thing in her mouth at once but lost a block of chocolate in the sand in the process. Logan got the burnt outside of the marshmallow into the s'more, but most of the center had stubbornly stayed on the stick.

"Amateurs!" said Gabby, shaking her head in disgust. "Watch and learn, Penny."

She slowly rotated her stick on the periphery of the fire until her two marshmallows were perfectly brown on all sides. In the meantime, she had asked Missy (who she referred to as her "apprentice") to prepare the rest of the s'more.

"The whole purpose of the 'slow burn,' or 'slow brown' as some call it, is that it is melted on the inside, so the heat from the marshmallow melts the chocolate while the graham crackers act as a buffer, and the whole thing becomes a gooey mess of deliciousness."

Willow was so intrigued with the s'more lesson in progress that she didn't notice when her own marshmallow burst into flames. By the time she realized, it was too late: it had dropped off her stick and plopped into the fire.

"See, Penny: that right there, that's what you *don't* want to do."

Willow looked at her stick, which just had a bit of melted marshmallow left on it.

"Oh no!" she cried. "Does anyone have more marshmallows?"

"So, the whole organic unrefined sugar thing, that's . . ."

"Officially suspended until camp is over."

"I'm going to tell the vegetarians on you."

"You wouldn't!"

"Willow, I was kidding."

"Oh. I mean, *obviously*. So, what's the 'mallow' status?"

"It's time to witness the greatness," yelled Gabby. "You are now looking at a perfectly browned marshmallow. Missy, are you ready to accessorize?"

"Ready!"

"Graham crackers," demanded Gabby.

Missy held out the two graham crackers.

"Chocolate."

Missy placed two rectangular blocks of Hershey's chocolate on each cracker.

"Marshmallows."

Gabby gently laid the marshmallows on top of one side,

and then Missy put the other cracker on top, gently bracing the browned 'mallow as Gabby carefully removed the stick.

"And *voilà*!" she said, holding up the stick for all to see. "See, girls? No residue!"

The other girls oo-ed and aah-ed, partly mocking, but mostly sincere. Penny deemed Gabby the Yoda of s'more making, because she took one bite of the delicious concoction, and suddenly everything was clear: if you put different things together that at first don't make sense, they may just make the best combination. But, as Gabby maintained, the whole process could not be rushed. It takes time and patience. This was one sweet campfire lesson that Penny would not forget.

That night, Penny Moore had her very first *real* s'more . . . and then her second, and then her third, and so *fourth*. The girls nicknamed her Penny S'Moore, and called her S'Moore for the rest of the evening. While Penny had to admit to feeling ill from all the sugar, she loved her new nickname. Because, as she was learning, nothing showed love at camp like a solid nickname . . . and a s'more made just for you by a camp friend.

After the girls gleefully rode through their s'more-induced sugar high with a spirited game of "duck, duck, goose"—which turned into "bat, bat, rabies!"—they went into their tents. Bunk One had been given strict and simple rules: go to sleep. But Penny, feeling untouchable in the rule-breaking arena, had an idea. The girls waited exactly one hour, and then signaled one another with a series of flashlight flickers. They were attempting Morse code, but no one really remembered (or knew in the first place) the actual code, so they were just flashing lights at one another for twenty minutes until Jade got out of the tent and gathered everyone. They snuck down toward the lake, threw off their pajamas and nightshirts and sweatpants and nightgownshirts and anything else they were wearing, and ran into the water . . . totally naked.

Now, Penny had never skinny-dipped before in her life (unless a bath counts as skinny-dipping, which she didn't think it did), and while the lake was freezing, there was something so wild and fun about the whole thing. The girls were all splashing one another, and Missy kept sticking her bare butt out of the water and singing "Doing the butt," while the girls told one another how slutty they were.

Missy was the first one out of the water, but instead of putting her clothes or her towel on, she ran back and forth along the beach. Now, running around naked—or at the very least, partially clothed—was not out of the ordinary for Missy, but still, after a minute or two, the girls had to comment.

"Hey, Slutty! We get the point that you're really comfortable with your body and all, but seriously . . . put some clothes on, would you?!"

"Um, you guys? Our clothes are gone!"

"What?"

"Is this a fake out?"

"No! I am so not kidding!"

As the rest of Bunk One emerged from the water, they realized that all their clothes were, indeed, gone.

The next day, clothes-less and towel-less, Bunk One had to walk back up the hill wrapped in their sleeping bags. It was swelteringly hot, so being covered in down sleeping bags was not ideal. Once they got back to Bunk One and changed into uniforms, they went to breakfast where the mystery was solved: their clothes were laid out neatly on the benches of Table One, each with a little handwritten note that said: "From your secret admirer."

"Did you girls have a fun beach sleepover?" Dirk the Jerk asked through a mouthful of orange eggs.

The girls were speechless. Dirk the Jerk sat back and smiled.

CAMP RULE #16

Fern Lake ladies do not ride on waterslides with boys.

The day before Visiting Day, Bunk One took their last annual trip to the Aquabogan.

"The Aquabogan?" Penny asked. "What's the big deal? It's just a water park, right?"

"Oh, it's not *just* a water park," said Gabby.

"It has millions of waterslides, wave pools, minigolf, and junk food stands," said Missy.

"In a word, it's Mecca," said Willow.

"Every age group gets to go there once each summer, and no matter how old we get, we can never say no to a waterslide."

"Or the fried dough!" said Gabby.

"But it's not just all about the waterslides—"

"Or the fried dough!" repeated Gabby.

"The Aquabogan is the hub of Maine camp activity. You never know which one we'll see there."

"Well . . ."

"Okay, specifically, you never know which *boys* camp you'll see there."

"Yeah, I mean, it's not like we want to fraternize with other girls camps."

"What, like Robin Dogs?"

"Or Camp Fugly?"

The girls didn't stop talking and cheering and laughing all the way to the Aquabogan. They would get truckers to honk their horns by making a pulling-arm gesture out of the window of the camp van. This kind of childish prank never seemed to get old for them, and considering it was all new to Penny, she was happy to be along for the ride.

"You guys, this is so much fun! I am having so much fun right now! I am living in the moment!" yelled Gabby.

"Hey, it's like that day, you know, when we were in Bunk One, and we went to the Aquabogan?" mocked Jade.

"Oh my God! Do you guys remember that day?" asked Tess, catching on.

"That day we made truckers honk their horns," said Willow.

"And I ate my paper bag lunch before we got there,"

said Gabby as she put her salt and vinegar potato chips into her peanut butter and jelly sandwich and took a big crunchy bite.

"I totally remember that day!" said Missy.

"Like it was today!" said Tess.

Penny laughed along with the girls. She truly wished that she had been there from the beginning, that she had experienced these summers filled with these moments and memories from the time she was eight. She would have liked to have seen Jade with cornrows, or Logan when she was young and overdosing on Flintstones vitamins. But most of all, Penny would have liked for Logan to have liked her, to not have ruined Logan's summer, and for both of them to be able to enjoy it . . . together. But clearly, that was not going to happen anytime soon.

When they arrived at the Aquabogan, the parking lot was packed with school buses, vans, and family cars. The girls got their ride tickets and continued to comment on every moment, periodically taking turns exclaiming, "Do you remember that day we were in Bunk One and we went to the Aquabogan?"

They played miniature golf, and went on all the water-slides (although Jade passed on the Yankee Ripper, which was very high and had a steep drop-off). They ate fried dough, another sweet delicacy that Penny had been deprived of her entire life.

"It's fried and it's sweet. What's not to like?" asked Gabby, who was on her second. "I'm not even hungry anymore! I just want to 'remember that day,' y'know?"

"It's called sensory recall," said Willow.

"Wow, really? Sensory recall is delicious!"

Even Willow couldn't say "no to the dough," which was not vegan by any means, nor could Tess, who had pretty much given up on her tennis diet altogether.

They flirted with the "slide-masters," the zinc-ed up guys who sat at the top of each ride in folding chairs. The slide-masters were uniformly "hot" and lazily soaked up the rays, barely watching as they told each girl it was safe to go down the slide. Penny had to admit that even she was a little humbled when she had to wait on line, so accustomed had she become to the preferential Bunk One treatment she received at camp.

Penny was anxiously waiting at the top of the Yankee Ripper when she felt a tap on her shoulder.

"Uh, Miss, please wait your turn," said the male voice.

Penny knew that voice. But . . . it couldn't be! She turned around to see Cameron standing right behind her.

"Cameron! Hi! I mean, *hi*. What are you doing here?"

"I have some buddies who are counselors at another camp around here. We all meet up on their day off."

"Next!" yelled the slide-master, without looking at the slide or the next sliders.

"We're going together," said Cameron to the slide-master.

"Hey, Cam, how's it going, buddy?"

"Oh, hey, man, didn't recognize you under all the zinc. Life is good. Can't complain."

"Who's your friend?"

"This is Penny."

"Hey, Penny."

The white-zinc-faced slide-master laughed loudly and stared at Penny lasciviously. She gave him a half smile, and then sat at the top of the slide, ready to put an end to this particular rude-dude-interlude. Penny overheard the slide-master whisper something to Cameron about "robbing the cradle."

Cameron just laughed, and then surprised Penny by sitting right behind her on the slide. He put his arms around her waist and his legs around her legs. Every hair on her body was standing up. He nuzzled her ear and said, "Ready, Penny?"

"Go ahead, lovebirds!" said the slide-master.

"Here we go!" said Cameron.

Penny couldn't believe this was happening. How was she suddenly plummeting down a waterslide with Cameron attached to her? *Was this kind of tandem sliding even safe?* And where did her friends go? She realized at that moment that being a part of camp and being a part of Bunk

One was so much more important and so much more fun than having a crush on this boy. Penny screamed all the way down the slide, and then got what felt like a gallon of water up her nose when they slid into the pool at the bottom.

Cameron came up from underneath the water and shook his head so that his long bangs stuck to his forehead and covered his left eye. *Okay, yes, fine, he was seriously cute.*

"Wanna go again?" he asked.

Penny scanned the water park, but didn't see Bunk One. Should she take another ride with Cameron? Should she try to find her friends? Her questions were answered for her when she heard the familiar sound of a Fern Lake cheer:

> *"Who's a Moose, who's a Moose*
> *Who's a big fat juicy Moose*
> *Mooooooooooooooose!"*

The girls were sitting at a picnic table eating more fried dough and dorking out with their thumbs in their ears and their hands open so that they would each look like a moose. Penny had to laugh.

"You know what," said Penny, "I should get back to my friends."

"Are you serious?"

"Yeah."

"Okay, if that's how you feel."

"See you later, Cameron," said Penny. "And thanks for the ride!"

Penny ran out of the water and toward Bunk One's picnic table without so much as glancing back at him. She pushed Tess over on the bench so that she could sit next to her.

"Penny! Where'd you go?"

"Just can't get enough of the Aquabogan!" said Penny.

"We thought you were with Logan. We haven't seen her either," said Tess.

"Yeah, because Logan really wants to spend quality time with me."

"Logan's just stubborn. You'll see. She'll come around," said Jade.

"She's very territorial. She always has been," said Willow.

"She's like a dog peeing on a hydrant to mark her territory!" said Missy.

"Ewww."

"She doesn't like change."

"Probably because she never had much of a family of her own, so her camp friends—us—and the camp, we're her family."

"She always seems pretty happy at school," said Penny.

"That's because she's school-Logan."

"You guys talking behind my back?"

Logan walked up to the group with her Juicy cover-up on over her bikini.

"Yes, but nothing bad, Lo-Wo."

"We were just saying that even though you're high maintenance and high-strung, you're worth it. Because you're the best friend a girl could have."

"Okay, girls!" yelled Annie, walking up to them with her own piece of fried dough in her hand and powdered sugar around her mouth. "Time to pack it in!"

Although their sunscreen was supposedly waterproof, every one of the Bunk One girls was burned to a crisp by the time they got on the bus to head back to camp.

"Now I know how fried dough feels," moaned Missy.

"Does that mean that if I put powdered sugar on you, you would melt in my mouth?" asked Gabby.

"I dunno. Give it a try."

"You guys, do you remember that day, when we went to the Aquabogan, and I tried to eat Missy?" asked Gabby.

"Oh, you mean that day that you went all cannibal at the Aquabogan? Totally!"

"Sit with me," Logan whispered to Penny. "I need to talk to you."

Penny climbed into the van after Logan and sat in the very back row with her while the other girls cheered and sang tirelessly ahead of them.

"I think we got off on the wrong foot," said Logan.

"Uh, you think? You told me you hated me the first day."

"I know. I'm sorry. I don't always deal with change well . . . especially when I have been counting on something my entire life."

"Well, I'm sorry I screwed up your summer."

"Oh, you didn't."

"Really? Wow, I am so happy to hear that, Logan, because I've felt so badly, and I was having fun but I really wanted you to—"

"Okay, shut it, Dork-Girl. Now listen up. We had a deal, did we not?"

"Well, yeah, but that was before I got to know everyone and before I knew what camp was all about."

"Oh really, and what's that?"

"Well, acceptance, for one."

"No. Camp is about tradition. Camp is the last place where a girl can still be a girl, whether she's eight or sixteen. Camp doesn't change. You can count on it every summer. But I wasn't prepared for you. And I always keep my promises. I said I would have you home by Visiting Day."

"Yeah, but Visiting Day is tomorrow."

"So, you might want to start packing."

"I'm not going home, Logan," protested Penny. "I tried your way and it didn't work. And now I want to stay. Can't you just accept that?"

"No, I'm sorry. I can't. I just can't. And that's why it would just break my heart to have to show these pictures to George."

"What pictures?"

Logan took out her digital camera and started scrolling through until she came to ten straight shots of Penny and Cameron on the waterslide together! There was even one of him whispering in her ear, which looked like he was kissing her.

"The last girl who was caught 'canoodling' with Cameron was sent home a disgrace. So I give you the choice: go home with your parents on Visiting Day because you're homesick and you hate FLC, or these pictures get out and you're *sent* home and you can write your college essay about your slutty sleepaway camp summer. The choice is yours. Either way, see you in September, '*S'Moore.*'"

Penny was speechless. She felt sick. She couldn't believe this was happening. Logan hated her so much that she would be willing to basically ruin her life to get her out of camp. Penny's chin started quivering. She knew what she had to do, but she wouldn't have a chance to call her parents before Visiting Day, so she would just have to convince them to let her leave when she saw them. And how would she explain it to Bunk One?

Logan moved up to the next row of the van and started singing and cheering with the rest of the girls. Penny remained in the back, silent and alone. She stared out the window and wondered how any single person could be as mean and calculating as Logan Worthe.

When they got back to camp, Penny sat silent and zombie-like in an Adirondack chair under the trees, trying to enjoy what would be her last FLC evening. She looked out at the waterfront, at the girls finishing their last period of water-skiing or tennis or lacrosse, and she knew she would miss this place and these girls. But she had no other choice. Logan Worthe had blackmailed her and she had to go home.

"Penny!" screamed Morgan, running up the hill.

Morgan's eye patch was gone, but just before she reached Penny, she tripped over her own foot and did a face-plant into the ground, nearly impaling herself with her tennis racket.

"I'm okay!" she yelled.

Before Penny could go to her, Morgan jumped up, threw her arms around Penny's neck, and sat on the armrest of her chair.

"I just got moved up a level in tennis and my parents are coming tomorrow and I got sailing as an activity in the morning which is great because then I can show them how I learned to sail although I keep getting hit in the head with the boom and they keep thinking I'm going to black out but I don't but I get a headache sometimes but it's worth it because sailing is super fun! And I love camp sooooo much!!! Are you excited to see your parents, Penny?"

"Yeah. I am."

"Do you love camp as much as I do?"

"I'm not sure, Morgan, how much do you love camp?"

"Soooo much!"

"Can I get back to you on that?"

"Sure. I never want it to end. And Penny?"

"Yeah?"

"I couldn't have done it without you. You were my first ever camp-friend."

"Thanks, Morgan. You were mine, too."

"And look at us now!" said Morgan. "Isn't this place beautiful? I have to go change for dinner. I'll see you later!"

Morgan sped off, barely missing the pole on the volleyball court, but running straight into the net face-first, which caught her and propelled her backward. She landed on her back.

"I'm okay!" she yelled, giving Penny the thumbs-up before jumping up and running back to her bunk.

Penny laughed to herself. She would miss Morgan, and she would miss Bunk One, and she would miss Fern Lake. She stayed seated until dinner. She barely ate and didn't talk much. Some of the girls asked her what was wrong, but she just said she wasn't feeling well. Logan, on the other hand, was in rare form, starting cheers, getting "a little bit rowdy," and leading the group once again.

Looking out behind all the bunks after dinner, all Penny could see were rows of bare legs being Nair-ed and shaved out of buckets in anticipation of Visiting Day. She could also hear the desperate cries of girls who had decided to wax their own legs, and inevitably ended up taking off several layers of flesh along with the wax and/or making a huge sticky mess. Missy had taken some Popsicle sticks from arts and crafts, and was using them with her waxing kit. The wax got all over the back steps of the bunk, which Willow then sat in by accident. Penny had to help Willow extricate herself from her shorts, which she left stuck to the stairs. And then Missy got the wax in her hair, so Jade had to cut her bangs, which ended up being zigzagged. Everyone told her that it looked great, and "totally punk rock," but they all agreed when she left the room that she looked like her head had gotten caught in a paper shredder.

Gabby explained to Penny that the night before Visiting Day there was a tradition of Bunk One leading as "animal farm." The theory was that no counselor would punish a camper right before parents arrived.

So, around midnight, Bunk One clamored by the front door of the bunk.

"On three," said Logan.

"One," said Jade.

"Two," said Gabby.

"Three!" said Willow.

And with that, the girls started yelling barnyard animal noises, and ran out of the bunk toward the flagpole. Penny followed, "moo-"ing halfheartedly. Girls from every bunk around the circle came running to the center of campus, laughing and screaming.

"Animal farm!"

"Mooooo!"

"Oink!"

"Naaaaaaaaaaaaaay!"

"Ruf-ruff!"

"Caw, caw!" yelled Gabby.

"Caw?" Penny asked.

"Yeah, you know, a parrot! Ca-caw!"

"What kind of farms are you going to?" asked Jade.

"There are no parrots on farms?"

"None that I know," Penny admitted.

"So, where do the parrots live?"

Penny didn't answer, as she was focused on touching the flagpole and getting back to the bunk without getting caught (not that it mattered anymore). But the point was, she really *didn't* want to get caught. She wanted to stay at camp. She touched the flagpole, quickly pivoted—slipping a bit on the dewy grass—and then sprinted back toward Bunk One. She had the bunk in her sights when she felt a firm grip on her wrist. She swung around, in mid-"moo," only to see Cameron right in front of her.

"Can I talk to you?" he asked.

"I'm kind of busy," said Penny.

"It's about today. It's about Logan."

Penny stopped. Now, she was listening.

"It will only take a second," he pleaded.

Cameron took her hand, and together, they ran behind the bunks, into the dark woods near the ropes course. Penny's mind was racing. Did he want to make out with her? Did he want to be her boyfriend? Was she going to get poison ivy? She was in her nightgownshirt and sweats, after all. She didn't even have bug spray!

Cameron stopped next to a wide tree stump. He crossed his arms over his chest and put one foot on the stump.

"I wanted to talk to you before I left," he said.

"Where are you going?"

"Alaska."

"Yeah, right!"

"No, honestly. I've always wanted to go. I'm going to work on a fishing boat. I just couldn't afford the plane ticket."

"Oh. Well, good luck with that."

"I'm sorry if I creeped you out today. I didn't mean to, I was just kidding around, you know."

"That's okay. I'm fine."

"The thing I really want to tell you is that . . . it was Logan's idea."

"What?"

"She told me to go on the slide with you and all that and didn't tell me why, but she bought my ticket to Alaska in exchange."

"And why are you telling me this?"

"Because I saw the look on your face after the slide and I felt bad. You're a good girl, Penny. You're not a rule breaker. You shouldn't be messed up in all this. And I don't know what Logan is up to, but I have a feeling that whatever it is, it's not going to earn her that spirit award anytime soon."

"That's for sure," said Penny.

"So, that's it. I've said my piece. And now, I'm out-y. But I wish you luck, Penny. And maybe give me a call when you turn eighteen?"

"Thanks, Cameron," said Penny. "Good luck to you, too."

"Later," he said. And with that, Cameron disappeared into the night.

Penny sat down on the stump in the darkness. She laughed out loud because, well, she was indeed . . . *stumped*.

Logan Worthe must have really hated her to go through all of this to get her to leave. To stay would be to endure embarrassment and more torture, and that was not what she wanted for the rest of her summer. But she had also learned a lot these last few weeks . . . about taking risks, challenging rules, and surprising herself in the process, and she believed that she couldn't leave camp without confronting Logan.

Penny walked quickly back to Bunk One, before she lost her nerve. When she got there, the lights were out, and most of the girls seemed to be asleep. Penny tiptoed over to Logan's bed and tapped her shoulder. Logan groaned. Penny tapped her shoulder again.

"What?" Logan asked, groggy and annoyed.

"Shh," said Penny. "I need to talk to you."

"Now?"

"Yes, now."

Logan groaned again but slowly got up out of bed and followed Penny out the back of the bunk. They stood by the clothesline, which Logan scrutinized.

"Ugh, here's my Juicy tank top I was looking for! That's so annoying, now it's all dew-y."

"I know, Logan."

"Know what?"

"I know that you paid off Cameron to be close to me at

the Aquabogan so that you could get those pictures and use them to make me go home."

"I don't know what you're talking about."

"It's a really crappy thing to do, Logan."

"I'm not admitting guilt, but . . . what are you going to do?"

"Well, I thought about telling the other girls in Bunk One."

"I would deny it."

"Who do you think they would believe in this case, Logan, you or me?"

Logan didn't answer.

"I'm going to leave tomorrow, Logan. I'm going to leave because I don't want to stay where I'm not wanted, not because I don't like camp. I *love* camp. I understand why you come back here every summer, and I'm just sorry that I didn't have the chance to experience it the way you did."

"You're really not going to say anything to Bunk One?"

"Nope. What's the point? If I stay, I have to live with someone who hates me for the next four weeks. It's been hard enough already. Life is too short. Good luck, Logan. I hope you guys have a great rest of the summer."

And with that, Penny went back inside Bunk One, and got into bed for her last night's sleep as a Fern Lake lady at Fern Lake Camp.

CAMP RULE #17

*Fern Lake ladies do not beg
their parents to take them
home on Visiting Day.*

At reveille the next morning, there was a mad rush
for the showers. Visiting Day was the most heavily showered day of the summer. Girls from everywhere ran to one
of the three campus showering locations. They were carrying
buckets of products, and wearing their flip-flops and towels
and robes. Girls who had had their hair braided were wearing shower caps.

Some towels and robes "disappeared" while their owners were showering. Penny shook her head as she walked on
the pebbly road from the shower to the back door of Bunk
One, and saw one girl running around wrapped in a shower
curtain. Her hair was full of shampoo and she was screaming dramatically, "My eyes! I'm blind!"

The guilty pranksters huddled in plain sight on their

bunk steps, laughing and wrapped in the victim's pink towel. Penny knew she would miss this.

Breakfast was bagels and cream cheese (a pre-Visiting-Day food bribe). Most of the girls were excited to see their parents, but Tess was noticeably nervous. There was an art show on Visiting Day, and Penny knew Tess was worried about the project she had put in the show. She thought her parents might be angry with her and wouldn't be able to appreciate her post-tennis efforts. She *was* injured, for crying out loud!

After breakfast and cleanup, chimes rang to announce assembly. Penny looked out the bunk window and saw parents already waiting at the head of campus. Screams of excitement were heard throughout the circle of bunks. Then, Penny spotted her parents. Her father's arm was around her mother, who was jumping up and down like a little girl. Penny's eyes filled up with tears. She had missed her parents. She loved her parents. How disappointed they would be when she told them that she just had to go home.

Girls waited outside their bunks as the flag was raised, and with even more spirit than usual (which was *a lot*), they held hands and ran toward the center of campus. The cheers were overlapping one another, but nobody seemed to mind. Even though Penny knew most of the cheers at this point, and had come to enjoy the daily preannouncement cheering ritual, she couldn't bring herself to go with the other girls. She sat on Annie's bed and watched from behind the screened window, just as she had done on the very first morning.

Once Stacy got the girls to sit down around the flagpole, she welcomed the parents, who were now completely visible to all the campers. Girls were waving and pointing. Parents were waving back and proudly pointing out their daughters to other parents. Most of them were toting coolers, bags of food, and other goodies. Penny watched as both her parents stood on their tiptoes and craned their necks to find her in the crowd. Little did they know, she wasn't there.

When Stacy dismissed the girls, there was a mad rush for the head of campus as parents and daughters ran to one another with open arms. Penny was waiting until there was enough of a crowd in front of Bunk One so that she could blend in, and no one would be able to tell that she had skipped assembly.

Penny watched as Willow hugged her parents. They had driven to Maine the night before from New York City, where they lived on Central Park West in an apartment that was also their psychiatrist offices.

Penny heard Gabby's parents before she actually saw them. When they came into view, they were wearing big T-shirts that said, MY DAUGHTER IS IN BUNK ONE AND ALL I GOT WAS THIS LOUSY T-SHIRT.

Missy's mother was wearing a tight top and had clearly had work done on her face in the last month, as it didn't seem to move much. Her lips were so puffy that Penny was afraid they might just explode by cookie line. Missy's father was equally well preserved.

Tess's parents stood five feet from each other and reservedly hugged Tess after she had limped slowly up to the head of campus to greet them. Her mother's hair was immaculate, even under her wide-brimmed hat. She wore a silk sundress and heels. Penny imagined that a woman like Tess's mom just never sweated.

Jade's parents had driven up from Boston and stayed in a little inn the night before. Her mother was an artist, and her father was the aforementioned proctologist. They seemed cool and tough in the very same way that Jade was.

Most of the Bunk One parents seemed to know one another after all the summers the girls had spent together. Seeing all these girls with their unique parents just reminded Penny what a motley crew this bunk was, and how, oddly, she thought she may have found a place in it that she would miss . . . but would they miss her?

One set of parents, however, was nowhere to be found: Penny watched Logan as she wandered aimlessly through the sea of reunited parents and campers. Logan hugged some of the other Bunk One parents and Penny overheard her repeating:

"My parents will be here. They're always late."

Stacy made a beeline for Logan, pulling her away from the crowd toward Bunk One. Penny, still sitting on Annie's bed, overheard Stacy telling Logan that her parents were stuck in St. Tropez, so they would not be able to make it in time for Visiting Day this year. Logan didn't seem surprised, but she didn't seem happy about it either. Stacy awkwardly tried to put her arm around her, but Logan shook it off and walked into Bunk One alone. Penny jumped up, and ran over to her cubby, trying to look busy.

At first, Logan must not have seen her because she quietly closed her shutter, and sat on the edge of her bed. And then Penny saw something she had never seen before: Logan Worthe started to cry. Penny didn't know what to do. She hated Logan. Logan Worthe was a terrible awful horrible person. But Logan Worthe was a girl who Penny had come to know, and she had come to know her as more than just the popular, perfect girl who most people saw. Penny knew that even though Logan wouldn't admit it, she was disappointed and hurt that her parents weren't there.

And then, a teetering can of spray deodorant crashed down from the top of one of the cubbies, and Logan looked up, seeing Penny. She quickly wiped away her tears.

"What are you doing here?"

"I was . . . packing!" Penny held up a uniform shirt as proof.

"Aren't your parents here?"

"Yeah, I'm just not really . . . ready to face them yet."

"But I thought you *loved* your parents?"

"I do. I just . . . all right fine, I don't want to tell them I'm leaving camp, and I don't want to spend the rest of the summer with them, no matter how cool they are . . . for parents."

"At least you have people to go home to. Mine didn't even bother coming."

"I'm sorry, Logan."

"Oh, you hate me. Who are you kidding?"

"Well, you haven't given me a lot to like about you, but . . . I wouldn't wish parents bailing on Visiting Day on anyone."

"Wow. You actually *are* a really nice person. I kind of thought it was all an act."

"I'm a nicer person than you."

"Touché."

Suddenly, sunlight filled the bunk as the front door opened.

"Penny? Penny!" yelled Penny's mom. "Our little Fern Lake lady! What are you doing in here?"

"We were looking all over for you, and every girl kind of looks the same because you're all dressed the same, and it's been so long . . ."

They ran over to Penny and hugged her. Penny looked over their shoulders at Logan, who was wiping away her residual tears and fixing her ponytail.

"Did you get taller?"

"You look beautiful."

"Okay, take a breath, let's all just breathe, people," instructed Penny.

Penny looked at Logan, who seemed to actually be smiling a little.

"Mom, Dad, this is—well, you know what, what the heck. This is my *friend*, Logan Worthe."

Logan stood up and went to shake hands, but Penny's parents were not hand-shakers, especially when meeting someone who was purportedly a friend of Penny's, so they both bear-hugged Logan. Penny got a kick out of the surprised expression on her face.

"And you were worried that no one would like you!" said Penny's mom.

"Logan, Penny was worried that she wouldn't fit in! Could you imagine that?"

"You are so killing me right now, guys," said Penny.

"What? What did we say?"

"Logan, where are your folks?" asked Penny's mom.

"Oh, *come on*!!!" said Penny. "I'm sorry, they have no filter!"

It seemed like Logan was actually amused watching Penny get so aggravated with her parents, and witnessing all the blatant faux pas.

"My parents couldn't make it," said Logan.

"That's terrible!" said Penny's dad.

"Are they okay?" asked Penny's mom.

"Here we go," said Penny.

"Yes, they're fine. I think they just missed their flight. It's okay. I'll see them in four weeks."

"Well, for today, we are your parents, too! Get annoyed with us, eat the food we bring, let us make fools of ourselves . . . do we have a deal?"

"Thank you," said Logan. "Sure, it's a deal. It was really nice to meet you guys. It's not easy, coming into Bunk One as a first-year camper. Penny was very brave."

And with that, Logan walked out the back door of the bunk.

"Well, she seems very nice," said Penny's dad.

"You guys are so clueless, it's ridiculous," said Penny.

"What? She's not nice?"

"She goes to Lakefield. She's, like, the most popular girl in the *world*."

"She seemed very normal to me."

"Funny that you have to go hundreds of miles to become

friends with someone you go to school with every day."

"Yeah. Hilarious," said Penny.

"So, who's this extra sweat suit for?" asked Gabby's father as the Steinberg family walked into the bunk followed by the rest of Bunk One and their parents.

"Oh! Thanks, Dad," said Gabby. "This is my friend, Penny."

Gabby pulled Penny over, and put her arm around her shoulders. She took the matching Bunk One sweatshirt and sweatpants from her father and passed it to Penny.

"Now you're really part of Bunk One," said Gabby.

All the girls came over as Penny inspected her new sweat suit like it was Joseph's Technicolor dream coat. On the leg of the sweatpants, it said BUNK ONE, and on the butt it said, S'MOORE.

Gabby gave her a big wet kiss on the cheek, just as Jade leaned toward her other ear and whispered just loudly enough that Gabby could hear her as well.

"Sweatshops," said Jade.

"Jade!" yelled Gabby.

Penny laughed, and thanked Gabby's parents, who hugged her. Penny's parents introduced themselves to everyone, and the parents started talking with and over one another, which was fabulous in its utter anarchy and volume. Tess's parents nodded instead of shaking hands or hugging anyone. Gabby's parents hugged everyone several times. Missy's parents spoke without their faces moving, which was interesting, and Penny was sure that Willow's parents were watching everyone and psychologically deconstructing the family dynamics. Penny took a step back from it, from all the girls, from all the parents, from all the Pringles and the Squeeze Cheese that was being unveiled, and she was so . . . sad. How could she leave all this? But she put on a happy face, and planned to take her parents aside later in the day and tell them the bad news.

The Bunk One girls and their parents sat in the Adirondack chairs under the trees all morning and chatted and caught up on the happenings of the summer. The parents lamented that none of the girls had written many letters that summer, and the letters they did write were pretty much grocery lists of what they needed delivered on Visiting Day. Nevertheless, all the parents just seemed happy to be reunited with their daughters. Logan, on the other hand, was missing.

After cookie line, the parents walked through the art show, looking at what the girls had done so far that summer, which, aside from Tess's project, was not much. They had been so busy simply being Bunk One that they just didn't make much time for the art show. The parents reminisced about the lanyards the girls used to make them, the ceramic mugs they proudly molded, and the collages and enameled jewelry they had toiled over in previous summers.

The only people who didn't seem to truly appreciate the art show were Tess's parents. Tess had constructed a huge Jackson Pollack-like oil painting on canvas. She had mixed the layers of paint with blades of grass, crumbs of Fern Lake cookies, smeared ice cream, blue stains of bug juice, bent utensils from her own mess kit, a piece of a shower curtain she had to wear when Bunk One had stolen her towel, green clay from the tennis court, and then, in the center of the large piece—stuck to the canvas with paint—was her very expensive and now semiretired . . . tennis racket. Tess's mother took one look at the painting, her lips barely parted as she tried to utter some words, but ultimately, she failed. Instead, her eyes rolled into the back of her head and she fainted into her husband's arms.

Tess bit her lip, as if trying not to cry. Penny went over and put her arm around her.

"Wow. Tess's mom does one hell of a trust fall," said Jade.

The girls shushed Jade.

"What?" she asked innocently.

"Could someone help me?" asked Tess's father.

The "earthy" pottery counselor, Ian Pottery, helped Tess's father move Tess's limp mother to a bench. Her legs fell open on either side. Willow was on her way to get help when Tess's mother got a direct whiff of Ian Pottery's armpit as he leaned over her. It seemed to have the same effect as smelling salts. She awoke with a startled breath, as if she had been underwater for an extended period of time.

Tess's father fanned his wife.

"We're taking you home, Tess. This is not the place for you. I'm sorry we ever sent you here. It was your father's idea."

"No," said Tess quietly.

"Excuse me?"

"No. I love it here. I have never been happier. It's not your life, Mummy. It's mine."

"Your father and I—"

"What? Don't make it seem like you're some united front . . . you barely talk to each other anymore. Or me."

Tess's mother sat up straight, looked around at all the Bunk One girls and their parents staring at her, and then stood uneasily.

"Let's go, Ronald."

"I'm not going. I came here to visit my daughter and I'm staying. Whether she's playing tennis or not."

"Well, then I'll be waiting in the car."

"For five hours?"

Tess's mother huffed and walked toward the parking lot. Tess's father put his arm around Tess and gave her a squeeze, just as chimes rang, signaling that it was lunchtime.

Lunch was a hot dog and hamburger cookout (luckily Dirk the Jerk's weiner was nowhere to be seen). Tess's mother rejoined the group on the softball field where everyone was sitting on the ground eating.

"It was too hot in the car," she said.

Tess smiled and offered her mother some of her hamburger.

"Wow," whispered Willow.

"What?" asked Penny.

"That is *huge!*"

"What's huge?"

"Well, according to Tess, no one in her family ever actually communicates about anything, so you have just watched some huge familial strides being taken today just by her mother returning to the regularly scheduled program."

"That's good, right?"

"Yes. It's good!" said Willow.

Penny was happy that Tess had resolved some of her family issues. She loved Tess and wanted her to be happy. Now Penny hoped that her issues would be resolved as easily.

One of the most important parts of Visiting Day was rest hour, when the girls hid the food that their parents had brought. They talked about how two summers before, they had hidden so much food—and had hidden it so well—that they forgot about half of it (and/or couldn't find it) and their bunk became infested by mice! They had to camp out for two days while the bunk was exterminated.

Penny hadn't had a moment to talk privately with her parents all day, and the day was half over already. So she pulled them outside the bunk (no counselor would dare bust a *parent* for bunk hopping!).

"Mom, Dad, there's something I need to talk to you about," said Penny.

"You're welcome," said Penny's mom.

"What?" asked Penny.

"You're welcome. You were going to thank us for sending you to camp, right? I mean, we've never seen you so happy, and that makes us happy. So it was a wonderful gift for us all. You're welcome!"

"Okay, yeah. I don't know how to say this."

"Just, say it."

"I need to go."

"What?"

"I need to leave with you guys. Today. This afternoon. It won't take me long to pack . . ."

"What are you talking about? Your bunk loves you, you love them . . ."

"It's not . . . it's complicated, guys. But, we had a deal, remember? You promised that if I wanted to go home on Visiting Day, if I tried camp for four weeks and I still didn't like it when you arrived, that you would take me home."

"But . . ."

"You promised!"

"I know, but . . ."

"Honey, we promised her. If Penny really wants to come home, then . . . we have no choice. We have to trust she has her reasons."

"What's wrong with you, Alan?"

"Honey . . ."

"But she's happy—"

"Hello! *She* is right here!" said Penny.

"Penny, is this really what you want?" asked Penny's dad.

"Yes," said Penny.

"Then go ahead and start packing. I'll talk to your mother out here."

"Alan!"

Penny walked into the bunk. Was that it? Was it that easy? Now, all she had to do was pack, and . . . leave. And it would be over. Fern Lake Camp would be just a distant memory. She wouldn't even get to be in the bunk picture. Penny started quietly gathering her belongings out of her cubby.

"Oh wait!" said Gabby. "Look at Penny. She's got a great idea!!! She seems to be taking out all her clothes in order to hide her food at the very bottom."

"How positively thorough!"

"Oh yeah, that's a great idea!" said Missy.

"And then, you can, like, weave the flatter items like Twizzlers and gum and Jolly Ranchers in between each shirt," said Gabby. "This is *geeeeeeeeeenius*! Nice work, Penny!"

"What did we do without you all these summers, Penny?" asked Tess.

The girls started taking piles of clothes out of their cubbies and dumping them on their beds.

"You guys, I'm not . . . I'm not hiding food," said Penny.

"Oh, is your mom making you reorganize your cubby?"

"My mom already reorganized mine!" said Missy.

"My mom remade my bed!" said Gabby.

"Well, what? Did you expect me to let my daughter sleep on this lumpy mess all summer?"

"I love my lumpy mess."

"No, you guys, I'm not hiding food or reorganizing. I'm . . . leaving."

"Leaving where?"

"Camp."

"What?"

"Why?"

There were gasps and cries.

"What are you talking about?"

"Why is the new girl leaving?"

"Her name is Penny, Mom!"

"Penny, you can't be serious."

"Penny, you can't go! You're one of us!"

Just then, Logan walked in through the back door of the bunk. Her eyes were red from crying and she didn't look like her normal put-together self at all.

"What's going on?" she asked quietly.

As if you don't know.

"Penny is leaving camp! She's going home!"

"It's a family emergency," said Penny.

The girls looked at each other gravely, knowing this was camp code for something else.

Penny looked at Logan. Her uniform didn't seem to fit so perfectly anymore, and there was something so utterly human and sad about her. The two girls stared at each other, enemies, until Penny caught the beginnings of a smile on Logan's face.

"FAKE OUT!" yelled Logan.

"What?"

"What the . . ."

"We totally got you guys!" said Logan. "Hey, guys, did you know *gullible* isn't in the dictionary?"

"Really?"

"Duh?"

Logan walked over to where Penny was standing, and put her arm around her.

"Nice work, Moore, I think we really got 'em."

"Yeah, we got 'em all right," said Penny, still piecing the events together.

"Let me help you put these clothes back into your cubby," said Logan.

"You guys are so annoying . . . that's not a funny fake out . . . I was really upset!"

"Wait, but, so gullible is or isn't in the dictionary? I'm so confused," said Missy.

Logan and Penny deposited piles of uniforms back into Penny's cubby. When they finished putting them on the shelves, they faced each other.

"I'm sorry," said Logan quietly. "I'm really . . . sorry. I hope you'll forgive me . . . and stay."

Logan placed something in Penny's hand. Penny held out her palm to see a tiny digital camera memory disc.

"Is this . . ."

"It's yours. Destroy it, do whatever you want with it. I'm really sorry, Penny."

Penny just smiled. And then Penny's mom stormed into the bunk, in tears. Penny's father followed immediately behind her.

"I am really not okay with this. Really. Not. Okay. But your father has assured me that we should let you do what you want to do, and I do not want to set the example as a promise breaker, but Penny, as your mother, I think you should stay."

"It's a fake out, Mom. Chill out."

"What? What? What's a fake out?"

"I think she's saying she was just kidding. It was fake: a fake out."

"It amazes me that you understand their lingo."

"It's a talent," said Penny's father.

"I don't know what it is, but I'm glad one of us gets it!"

CAMP RULE #18

Once a Fern Lake lady, always
a Fern Lake lady.

Visiting Day flew by . . . and Penny was still there!
Campers of every age were saying good-bye to their parents:
some were crying; some were visibly using all their will to
restrain the waterworks; and some gave their parents quick
hugs, and ran back to their bunks to make sure none of
their Visiting Day loot had been discovered.

It was difficult for Penny to say good-bye to her parents
because she really loved them and would miss them. And
she knew it must have been hard for them to leave, too. But
she was thrilled and relieved that she was staying.

She watched them walk up to the parking lot from her
place with other campers behind the small chain dividing
the camp from Fern Lake Road. Her parents kept turning
back and waving until they got in their car, and honked as
they drove away.

Penny started walking back to the bunk, thinking about what a bizarre day—what a bizarre month—it had been! She felt like she had grown ten years . . . by just being a kid again.

"Did you have a good Visiting Day?" asked Logan, sneaking up behind her.

"Yeah. Yeah, I did."

"You ready for another four weeks, S'Moore?"

"Ready as I'll ever be."

"Good."

"Hey, Logan?"

"Yeah?"

"Can I ask you *two* questions?"

"Yeah."

"You totally think I'm cool."

"What? That's not even one question!"

"Just admit it, Lo-Wo, you totally love Dork-Girl! You so want to be my camp friend."

"You're crazy, S'Moore. I think all the Laffy Taffy you ate went to your head."

"Oh yeah, we'll see about that."

"Slutties!!!" yelled Jade and Missy.

"Hi, Slutties!"

"I have tomatoes . . . from my garden," gushed Willow.

"My parents said I could take art classes when I get

home," said Tess. "Although, I'll have to babysit for the rest of my life in order to pay for the tennis racket."

"Wah-waaaaaaaaaaaaaaaah!" they yelled.

There was a big bonfire on the beach that night. The girls sang songs through mouthfuls of s'mores. Penny had a stick in each hand and was browning her marshmallows to perfection, if she did say so herself.

"I'm gonna need some stuff! Who's got my back?" she yelled.

"I've got it," said Logan.

She moved toward Penny with the open-faced graham cracker and chocolate sandwich.

"This one's for you, Lo-Wo," said Penny. "It's a S'Moore s'more."

"Oh, no! I couldn't."

"Okay, then I'll eat it."

"On second thought . . ."

"I thought so."

"I've created a monster!" said Gabby.

"You haven't seen anything yet," said Penny. "I'm just getting started."

After the bonfire, all the campers made a circle around the flagpole with their arms crossed, right over left, holding one another's hands as they had done on the first night of camp. But now, Penny stood with her beloved Bunk One, clinging to them as tightly as they did to her. And she knew every word to every song, which she sang proudly.

Penny looked up—past the flag blowing in the wind, past the towering pines swaying in the night, up toward the bright starlit sky.

"You know what they say?"

"No, what do they say, Logan?"

"Once a Fern Lake lady, always a Fern Lake lady."

"Now that's one camp rule I would never break," said Penny.

The girls continued singing together until their voices became just an echo reverberating throughout Fern Lake Camp.

ABOUT THE AUTHOR

Long before native New Yorker Jordan Roter moved to Los Angeles to work in film development and production, she spent six glorious summers at sleepaway camp.

Visiting Day was an annual ritual for Jordan, seen here at Tripp Lake Camp with her father. Jordan says, "For the record, my dad was not *actually* playing tennis that day, it was just 1985."

You can learn more about Jordan and her own years as a camper at www.jordanroter.com